大学英语泛听

4

EXTENSIVE LISTENING for COLLEGE STUDENTS

主　编：刘　成　肖　飞
副主编：唐国跃　史伏荣　顾琦一

外语教学与研究出版社
FOREIGN LANGUAGE TEACHING AND RESEARCH PRESS

(京)新登字155号

图书在版编目(CIP)数据

大学英语泛听4/肖飞,刘成主编. -北京:外语教学与研究出版社,2002

ISBN 7-5600-3035-1

Ⅰ.大… Ⅱ.①肖…②刘… Ⅲ.英语-听说教学-高等学校-教学参考资料 Ⅳ.H319.9

中国版本图书馆CIP数据核字(2002)第069065号

大学英语泛听 4
主　编:肖　飞　刘　成
*　*　*
责任编辑:赵东岳
出版发行:外语教学与研究出版社
社　址:北京市西三环北路19号(100089)
网　址:http://www.fltrp.com.cn
印　刷:江苏省常熟市华通印刷有限公司
开　本:787×1092　1/16
印　张:13.25
版　次:2004年6月第2版　2005年6月第5次印刷
书　号:ISBN 7-5600-3035-1/G·1457
定　价:16.90元
*　*　*

《大学英语泛听》编委会

前　言

大学英语的教学目标是培养学生英语综合应用能力，特别是听说能力，使他们在今后工作和社会交往中能用英语有效地进行口头和书面的信息交流，同时增强其自主学习能力、提高综合文化素养,以适应我国经济发展和国际交流的需要。为了适应我国高等教育新的发展形势，深化教学改革，提高教学质量，满足新时期国家和社会对人才培养的需要，根据国家教育部《大学英语课程教学要求》的规定，外语教学与研究出版社组织编写了《大学英语泛听》。

《大学英语泛听》力求体现一个“泛”字。一是选材“泛”, 涉及日常生活、社会习俗、体育、教育、择业、历史、文化、艺术、经济、法律、最新科技等方方面面。二是内容形式“泛”，包含有简短对话、情景对话、短文、幽默故事以及各种形式的练习。三是适用范围“泛”，它可用于课堂教学，也可用作第二课程使用，创造英语学习环境，活跃校园英语学习气氛。另外，虽然《大学英语泛听》主要是为非英语专业大学生设计的，但它也适用于英语专业低年级大学生和其他英语自学者。

《大学英语泛听》力求集知识性、趣味性、时代性、可听性和可模仿性于一体。

1. 知识性：每一单元围绕一个主题展开，并包含了相关知识的介绍，内容涉及从日常生活到最新科技等方方面面。
2. 趣味性：在内容、语言、版式、和插图等方面都力求趣味性，每一单元都附有小幽默或故事，让学习者在提高英语听说能力的同时得到精神上的享受。
3. 时代性：在教材上注意选择了不少体现时代气息的主题，同时在语言上也力求贴近时代发展的特点。
4. 可听性：考虑到听的特殊要求，在词汇数量和难度、句子长度和难度以及总体上都作了适当控制，同时，各册和每册各单元的次序安排上都仔细考虑到难度梯度。
5. 可模仿性：力求体现现代英语教学的有关理论和方法，通过大量的真实实用的语言输入，给学习者提供良好的模仿机会，并为学习者用英语表达自己的思想打好坚实的基础。

《大学英语泛听》的录音磁带和光盘由外国专家和专业技术人员共同录制，其语音纯美、地道、清晰。

本册各单元编者分别为：肖飞（1-12对话部分），唐国跃（1、12）；季月（2、4、5、）；刘成（3）；史伏荣（6）；顾琦一（7、10、11）；章丽君（8）；吴雪云（9）。

《大学英语泛听》的编者们恳请使用者对本书中出现的问题提出宝贵的意见和建议，以便再版时改进。

《大学英语泛听》编委会

2004 年6月

CONTENTS

LEARNERS' TEXTBOOK

Unit One Education

Part One Short Conversations

Listen to the following short conversations and choose the best answer to each question you hear.

1. A. Two dollars. B. Five dollars.
   C. Three dollars. D. Seven dollars.
2. A. 35 miles an hour. B. 55 miles an hour.
   C. 75 miles an hour. D. 95 miles an hour.
3. A. 4 pounds. B. 6 pounds. C. 8 pounds. D. 10 pounds.
4. A. 11:00. B. 12:00. C. 1:15. D. 11:45.
5. A. 2. B. 5. C. 7. D. 9.
6. A. 10 cents. B. 5 dollars. C. 50 cents. D. 25 cents.
7. A. $3.00. B. $3.75. C. $3.25. D. $4.00.
8. A. $0.40. B. $0.45. C. $0.35. D. $0.30.
9. A. The speed limit was not clearly marked.
   B. The limit was clearly marked as 40 miles per hour.
   C. The speed limit is 30 miles per hour.
   D. 50 miles per hour is the speed limit.

10. A. He is 61. B. He is 62. C. He is 64. D. He is 60.

11. A. He works three times as much as he did before.
    B. He has two free days for every three days he works.
    C. He works three nights every two weeks.
    D. He has twice as much work as he used to have.

12. A. The bus has broken down and will not arrive.
    B. The bus was in a terrible accident.
    C. The bus will probably arrive at 9:15.
    D. The bus may arrive tonight, but the man isn't sure.

13. A. 15. B. 50. C. 85. D. 100.

14. A. Two hours. B. Less than an hour.
    C. Thirty minutes. D. More than an hour.

15. A. It will be ready at four o'clock today.
    B. It can be picked up at two o'clock tomorrow.
    C. It will be ready in two hours.
    D. Only two rolls will be ready on time.

Part Two Dialogue

Education in Canada

Words and Expressions

tertiary	/'tәːʃәri; (*US*)-ʃieri/	*adj.*	高等的；第三级的
board	/bɔːd/	*v.*	寄宿
boarding	/'bɔːdiŋ/	*n.*	寄膳宿
eligible	/'elidʒәbl/	*adj.*	有资格的；合格的
vocational	/vәu'keiʃәn(ә)l/	*adj.*	行业的，职业的
Ontario	/ɔn'tεәriәu/	*n.*	安大略
Quebec	/kwi'bek/	*n.*	魁北克
liberal arts			文科

1. Listen to the dialogue and decide whether the following statements are true (T) or false (F).

( ) 1) Education in Canada is compulsory from ages 5 to 16.

( ) 2) Secondary school lasts from grade 9 to grade 12.

( ) 3) There are two streams in high school in Canada, sciences and liberal arts.

( ) 4) University entrance may be gained both from academic and commercial streams.

( ) 5) Private schools often offer better education than public schools do.

( ) 6) Those who are ineligible can pay to go to university in Canada.

( ) 7) Students in Canada usually begin their post-secondary education at the age of 17 or 18.

( ) 8) In Quebec, thirteen years of study is required before going to universities.

2. Listen to the last part of the dialogue and fill in the blanks with the information you hear.

In general, they enter post-secondary education at the age of 17 or 18, after 11 or 12 years of 1) ____________. But in Ontario, 2) ____________ of study is required. In Quebec, though students complete secondary schooling 3) ____________, those who wish to 4) ____________ must first take a 2-year pre-university program at a college of 5) ____________.

3. Discuss with your partner about the educational system in Canada and compare it with Chinese educational system.

Part Three Compound Dictation

Guides to American Universities

Listen to the passage and fill in the blanks with the information you hear.

Do you intend to study at an American university? It takes a long time to get 1) ________ ________ at most American schools, perhaps as much as a year. That's why you should start 2) ________________ a school as soon as possible. It's also a good idea to 3) ________ ________ to several different institutions, so that you'll have a 4) ________________ chance of acceptance at one.

There are two good ways to get the 5) ________________ you need. One is a general 6) ________________ book called *Guide to American Colleges and Universities*. The other is the 7) ________________ published by each school. 8) ________________ ________________________________. This book has many useful statistics, such as the number of students, the average test scores for people accepted to the school, the number of books in the library and the number of faculty members.

9) ____.
For instance, many schools raise their tuition every year. Also, schools sometimes change their requirements for entrance. To be sure that you are getting current information, write to the university and ask for its catalogue. 10) ________________________________ ____.
For instance, the catalogue can tell you if there is a special foreign student adviser, what kind of housing is available.

Part Four Passages

A. College Education in Britain

Words and Expressions

compulsory	/kəm'pʌlsəri/	*adj.*	义务的
automatically	/ˌɔːtə'mætik(ə)li/	*adv.*	自动地
assessment	/ə'sesmənt/	*n.*	评估；评价
grant	/grɑːnt/	*n.*	授给物（如补助、拨款等）
accommodation	/əˌkɔmə'deiʃ(ə)n/	*n.*	住处

Cambridge University

1. Listen to the passage and decide whether the following statements are true (T) or false (F).

(　) 1) Most students live on the university campus.

(　) 2) Most students attend a university which is away from their hometown.

(　) 3) Local education authorities award grants to students.

(　) 4) The grants are given on the basis of their marks.

2. Listen to the passage again and fill in the blanks with the information you hear.

1) Education is compulsory in Britain ____________.
2) Most students usually spend ____________ in universities.
3) Students studying modern languages spend ____________.
4) Students studying medicine spend ____________.
5) Entry to university is competitive and simply obtaining a pass in your "A" level examinations does not automatically ____________.
If you are successful in your interview, the university ____________
____________.

3. Talk with your partner about the educational systems in Canada, America, and Britain according to what you hear in this unit.

Oxford Graduation

B. Problems with US Education

Words and Expressions

peg	/peg/	*v.*	固定；限制
get boxed in			钳制；封锁
be tracked into			(美)按成绩分组(分班)
standardized test			标准化考试
be conducive to			有助于
be geared towards/to			适合……
be well rounded			全面的

1. Listen to the passage and choose the best answer to each of the following questions.

1) What did the speaker plan to do when he was in college?

A. To become a teacher.

B. To become a lawyer.

C. To be an engineer.

D. To be an artist.

2) Why did he change his original plan?

A. Because he was in another direction.

B. Because he came to realize that the educational system hinders students' development in a sense.

C. Because he is changeable.

D. Because he found it not interesting.

3) What did he remember about his elementary as well as secondary education?

A. The way that students were treated.

B. The way that students were put in the box.

C. The way that students were punished.

D. The way that students got boxed in.

4) Which of the following is NOT true according to the speaker?

A. A lot of people who are very intelligent have more opportunities.

B. A lot of decisions are really made for you.

C. The speaker disagrees with a lot of ways in the educational system.

D. The students had more pressure.

5) What can you infer from the talk about education in USA?

A. People can get into good colleges so long as they are intelligent and brilliant.

B. The educational system aims to develop people's special interest.

C. We cannot judge people simply because of scores on a standardized test.

D. The school system was conducive to students.

2. Listen to the passage again and fill in the blanks with the information you hear.

Uh ... people don't seem to recognize 1)_____________________________, they seem to just want to give 2)____________________ and peg you down to 3)____________________. And I think there are a lot of people, who are very intelligent, that I've known 4)____________________, have not had a lot of 5)____________________ if the school system was more conducive to students ... learning ... 6)____________________. I've always felt that a lot of classes that you're forced to take in high school are not really geared towards 7)_____________________________. There's very little emphasis on 8)____________________. Uh ... everybody's sort of treated like they're the same person.

3. Discuss US education with your partner and talk with him or her about the problems in your educational system.

Unit Two Human Qualities

Part One Short Conversations

Listen to the following short conversations and choose the best answer to each question you hear.

1. A. A clerk at the airport information desk.
   B. A clerk at the railway station information desk.
   C. A policeman.
   D. A taxi-driver.
2. A. A guest and a receptionist.
   B. A passenger and an air hostess.
   B. A customer and a shop assistant.
   D. A guest and a waitress.
3. A. Librarian and student. B. Operator and caller.
   C. Boss and secretary. D. Customer and repairman.
4. A. A writer. B. A teacher. C. A reporter. D. A student.
5. A. In a hotel. B. At a dinner table.
   C. In the street. D. At the man's house.
6. A. Relatives. B. Roommates. C. Colleagues. D. Neighbors.

7. A. A student. B. A reporter.
   C. A visitor. D. A lecturer.
8. A. To the school. B. To a friend's house.
   C. To the post office. D. Home.
9. A. A shop assistant. B. A telephone operator.
   C. A waitress. D. A clerk.
10. A. A railway porter. B. A bus conductor.
    C. A taxi driver. D. A postal clerk.
11. A. They are twins. B. They are classmates.
    C. They are friends. D. They are colleagues.
12. A. Looking for a timetable. B. Buying some furniture.
    C. Reserving a table. D. Window shopping.
13. A. In a cotton field. B. At a railway station.
    C. On a farm. D. On a train.
14. A. A teacher and a student. B. A patient and a doctor.
    C. Two friends. D. A husband and wife.
15. A. At the hospital. B. At the library.
    C. At the bakery. D. At a restaurant.

Part Two Dialogue

I Think You're in the Wrong Place

Words and Expressions

queue	/kjuː/	*n. & vi.*	行列；排队
barge	/baːdʒ/	*vi.*	闯入；冲
contradict	/ˌkɔntrə'dikt/	*vt.*	同……矛盾；反驳
brawl	/brɔːl/	*vi.*	争吵；对骂
push in			推进；插入
tear the feathers out of one's hat			杀某人的嚣张气焰

1. Listen to the dialogue and choose the best answer to complete the following sentences.

1) People stood in the long line ________.

A. to buy daily necessities

B. to visit the museum

C. to pass the Customs

D. for an unspecified purpose

2) One lady tried to barge in front of other people because ________.

A. she was threatened

B. she made a mistake

C. she was reluctant to queue up and wait for her turn

D. she had right to stay where she wished

3) What would the other lady probably do by saying "I'll tear the feathers out of your hat!"?

A. To force the queue jumper to queue up.

B. To leave the queue with her.

C. To use severe words.

D. To tear the other lady's hair.

4) The lady who pushed in was ________.

A. courteous

B. warmhearted

C. rude

D. honest

2. Listen to the dialogue again and fill in the blanks with the information you hear.

***Lady A*:** Excuse me, but I think you're in the wrong place.

***Lady B*:** Are you speaking to me?

***Lady A*:** Yes. The end of the queue's 1) ________________. I Think you've made a mistake.

***Lady B*:** A mistake. I have the right to 2) ________________.

***Lady A*:** Maybe. But you have no right to 3) ________________ in a queue.

***Lady B*:** Barge, did you say?

***Lady A*:** Yes. We've all been waiting here for 4) ________________.

***Lady B*:** Well, so have I.

***Lady A*:** Look. I don't like to contradict you but you weren't here 5) ________________.

***Lady B*:** I have no intention of 6) ________________. Here I am and I intend to stay.

***Lady A*:** Oh, no, oh no you can't stay. Other people here 7) ________________ too. Now get back to the end of the queue.

***Lady B*:** I have every right to stay wherever I like. It's a free country, isn't it?

***Lady A*:** Clever, very clever. 8) ________________. Well, let me tell you, you get out of this queue and move to your proper place at the back, or I'll tear the 9) ________________!

***Lady B*:** Are you threatening me?

***Lady A*:** That's right. And I always 10) ________________.

3. Questions for discussion.

1) What do you think of the lady who barged in front of a lot of people in the queue?

2) What would you do if you encountered people just like her?

Part Three Compound Dictation

Self-reliance

Listen to the passage and fill in the blanks with the information you hear.

Americans believe that individuals must learn to rely on themselves or risk losing freedom. This means 1) ______________ both financial and emotional independence from their parents as early as possible, 2) ______________ by age 18 to 21. It means that Americans believe they should take care of themselves, solve their own problems, and 3) ______________ on their own feet.

The strong 4) ______________ in self-reliance continues today as a 5) ______________ American value. This is perhaps one of the most difficult 6) ______________ of the American character to understand, but it is 7) ______________ important. Americans believe that they must be self-reliant in order to keep their freedom. 8) ____.

By being dependent, not only do they risk losing freedom, but also risk losing the respect of their peers (同辈人). 9) ____. In order to be in the main stream of American life — to have power and respect — an individual must be seen as self-reliant. Although receiving financial support from charity, family or the government is allowed, it is never admired. 10) ____.

Part Four Passages

A. The Four Qualities of Leadership

Words and Expressions

rugged	/'rʌgid/	*adj.*	粗犷而朴实的；粗野的
embrace	/im'breis/	*vt.*	拥抱；包含
redeem	/ri'diːm/	*vt.*	拯救；补偿
wilderness	/'wildənis/	*n.*	荒野
prosperous	/'prɔspərəs/	*adj.*	繁荣的；兴旺的
compel	/kəm'pel/	*vt.*	强迫，迫使
enlist	/in'list/	*v.*	征募，征召
unshakable	/ʌn'ʃeikəb(ə)l/	*adj.*	坚定不移的；不可动摇的
compensate	/'kɔmpenseit/	*v.*	补偿；赔偿
integrity	/in'tegriti/	*n.*	正直；诚实
seedtime	/'siːdtaim/	*n.*	播种季节；发展或准备的时期
Texas	/'teksəs/	*n.*	得克萨斯州(美国)
Stephen Fuller Austin			史迪文·夫勒·奥斯丁

1. Listen to the passage and give ticks (✓) to the qualities of leadership according to what you have heard.

( ) 1) sympathy
( ) 2) generosity
( ) 3) integrity
( ) 4) justness
( ) 5) devotedness
( ) 6) self-confidence
( ) 7) modesty
( ) 8) vision
( ) 9) conversable
( ) 10) ability to learn
( ) 11) enthusiasm for public utilities
( ) 12) aptness at expressing one's ambition

2. Listen to the passage again and answer the following questions.

1) What was the vision of Stephen Austin?

2) How did he tell others about his vision?

3) What was his attitude towards mistakes?

4) What did people in Texas think of him?

B. Diana, Princess of Wales

Words and Expressions

barrier	/'bæriə/	*n.*	障碍物；屏障
taboo	/tə'buː/	*n.*	(宗教方面的)禁忌、避讳
belie	/bi'lai/	*vt.*	掩饰，给人以……假像
landmine	/'lændmain/	*n.*	[军]地雷
highlight	/'hailait/	*vt.*	以强光照射；突出；强调
appalling	/ə'pɔːliŋ/	*adj.*	令人震惊的；骇人听闻的
left-over	/'left,əuvə/	*n.*	剩余物
consciousness	/'kɔnʃəsnis/	*n.*	意识，知觉，感觉
allied	/'ælaid/	*adj.*	同盟的；相关的
captivate	/'kæptiveit/	*vt.*	迷住；强烈感染
Bosnia	/'bɔzniə/	*n.*	波斯尼亚(南斯拉夫)
Diana			戴安娜
Princess of Wales			威尔士王妃
make a point of			强调；重视
walks of life			行业；职业

1. Listen to the passage and complete the following chart.

When	Where	What
1987		
1990s	…	
in the month of her death		

2. Listen to the passage again and fill in the blanks with the information you hear.

1) She was not just revealing one of her many ______________. This also showed her willingness to ______________ between people; and even to ______________.
2) She was ______________ in the world. Yet belying her image as ______________, she supported causes regarded by many as anything but fashionable and, with ______________, transformed perceptions of these.
3) And it was her commitment to other often overlooked causes such as ______________, homelessness, drugs and ______________ that had a similar impact on ______________.
4) She was an ______________ who could relate to people of all ages and from ______________.

3. Questions for discussion.

1) Why did Diana shake hands with AIDS patients?
2) Do you think Diana is somewhat different from other members of the British royal family? State your reasons.
3) What is your attitude towards the tragic death of Diana? Please talk with your partner.

Unit Three Management

Part One Short Conversations

Listen to the following short conversations and choose the best answer to each question you hear.

1. A. She went visiting with her husband.
   B. She hadn't expected to see Ted's father.
   C. One of Ted's parent wasn't at home.
   D. Ted saw both his parents today.
2. A. She feels that the trip will take too long.
   B. The students haven't chosen a professor.
   C. Prof. Smith has to choose the destination first.
   D. It's not certain the trip will take place.
3. A. Harvey doesn't like fish.
   B. Harvey doesn't belong here.
   C. Harvey wants some water.
   D. Harvey needs to go to class.
4. A. The man is always eating.
   B. She agrees with the man.

C. She wants him to tell her what he ate.

D. This is the second time the man said that.

5. A. He doesn't want to help.

B. He isn't able to work.

C. He will help the man later.

D. He'd like to work here.

6. A. Bill repaired the tire himself.

B. Bill paid to have his motorcycle fixed.

C. Bill was silly to have wasted his money.

D. Bill now works in a garage.

7. A. He must hand in a full report on the museum.

B. He is too busy to go along.

C. He has to wash his hands first.

D. He has already seen the whole museum.

8. A. She doesn't know how long they'll have to wait.

B. They're going to be in Washington at eight o'clock.

C. They're going to be very late.

D. The train doesn't go near Washington.

9. A. He isn't a talented writer.

B. He is a publisher.

C. He never thought such a thing would happen.

D. He was surprised to learn Jerald Brown was a talented writer.

10. A. The weatherman is usually accurate in his forecast.

B. The weatherman is usually inaccurate in his forecast.

C. It will be sunny all day.

D. It will be raining all day.

11. A. The neighbours probably won't turn down the music.

B. He should move to another place.

C. He wants to listen to different music.

D. He doesn't think the music is particularly loud.

12. A. He would like some help.

B. There's only one point he doesn't understand.

C. He can't learn the material.

D. These problems won't be on the exam.

13. A. She is afraid he can learn much.

B. She is afraid it's a waste of time.

C. She thinks it will be all right.

D. She is afraid he can't learn much.

14. A. He works very carefully.
    B. He received a traffic ticket.
    C. He always drives through a lot of traffic.
    D. He was offered a better job.
15. A. He might get lost in the crowd.
    B. He won't want to speak at the meeting.
    C. He doesn't like to go to other places.
    D. He has to go to another meeting first.

Part Two Dialogue

I Want A Change

Words and Expressions

downsize	/'daunsaiz/	*v.*	精简
benefit	/'benifit/	*n.*	福利
whim	/wim/	*n.*	幻想；怪念头
pink slip			粉红色通知(解雇通知)
employment agency			职业介绍所
on a temporary basis			临时的
with your attitude and ability			以你的态度和能力

1. Listen to the dialogue and decide whether the following statements are true (T) or false (F).

(　) 1) The man has been out of work five times in the past three years.

(　) 2) Although the man feels it is more secure for him to work in a company, he still looks forward to more freedom.

(　) 3) One of the man's friends just takes temporary jobs and makes more money and has more freedom.

(　) 4) The man is eager to follow the lead of his friends.

(　) 5) A lot of people dream of being their own boss.

(　) 6) The bad part of being his own boss is that he won't have all the benefits that go with working for a company.

2. Listen to the dialogue again and fill in the blanks with the information you hear.

Woman: I read that your company is downsizing again. What will that mean for your job?

Man: It means I'm 1) ________________. They have already given me a "pink slip".

Woman: That's 2) ________________. This has happened to you before, hasn't it?

Man: Yes. This will be 3) ________________ and I'm ready to call it quits.

Woman: What do you mean? You're going to 4) ________________?

Man: No, I'll still be working, but not for a company. I'm going to be 5) ________________.

Woman: Doesn't that make you 6) ________________? You won't have all the benefits that go with working for a company — no retirement, no 7) ________________.

Man: That is the bad part of it, but I am really 8) ________________ on the whims of big business. It seems that it hasn't been all that secure for me.

Woman: What will you do?

Man: I've had a couple of friends who have gone out 9) ________________. They say it is the best thing that ever happened to them.

Woman: I know it is the secret dream of a lot of people to be their own boss, especially 10) ________________.

Man: One of my friends just takes temporary jobs. Companies are looking for people with his skills, but only 11) ________________. So he goes from one company to another, depending on 12) ________________. He's able to set his own working hours and he makes a lot more than he did when he was working full time. He really likes 13) ________.

Woman: What does he do when he doesn't have any jobs coming in?

Man: He goes to a temporary 14) ________. It seems he always finds work and at double what he used to make.

Woman: I hope you find just the right thing for your skills. It would be nice to have a job that 15) ________.

Man: That's why I'm making the change. I want to be able to spend the extra time with my family.

Woman: Good luck! 16) ________, I'm sure you'll do well.

3. Do you want to be employed or do you want to set up your own business and work on your own after your graduation? Why?

Part Three Compound Dictation

Big Lesson from McDonald's

Listen to the passage and fill in the blanks with the information you hear.

Almost everywhere you go around the world, you see the famous McDonald's "Golden arches" and the 1) ________ figure of Ronald McDonald. Indeed, it has become a part of our lives.

The McDonald's 2) ________ in each market brings a new kind of 3) ________ for kids, teenagers, families, and working people. The restaurant offers good quality and highly 4) ________ fast food. The people behind each McDonald's 5) ________ may be young or old, but most of them are enthusiastic, 6) ________, polite and efficient.

It must be the way McDonald's recruits (招聘) and trains its employees that makes them shine (出众，超群) over other 7) ________ workers.

8) ____

____________________________________, learning about customer service, food retailing, food preparation, hygiene standards, health and safety issues, security and other food-related issues.

All this training is done on the job. On top of that, McDonald's offers no-obligation scholarships to assist employees in their external education.

9) ____

____

____________________________________.

Such training conditions the staff in the right attitudes — respect for customers and colleagues, and responsibility in doing a good job, no matter how menial it may seem. 10) ____

____

____________________________________.

Part Four Passages

A. Management and Culture

Words and Expressions

management style	管理模式
cultural differences	文化差异

Mitsubishi	三菱公司
Hitachi	日立公司

1. Listen to the passage and decide whether the following statements are true (T) or false (F).

( ) 1) Although the history and culture of Japan is different from the history and culture of Western countries, their management styles are quite similar.

( ) 2) In Japan, children feel strongly about the individual's position.

( ) 3) Westerners don't feel as strongly as the Japanese do about their companies.

( ) 4) Differences in opinion are not encouraged in Japan.

( ) 5) Japanese culture is a little better than Western culture.

2. Listen to the passage again and complete the following chart.

Differences in Management Style		
	Japan	**Western Countries**
Employee's Feelings towards the Company	The Japanese feel strongly about the company.	1)
Decision Process	2)	On the contrary, decisions in Western countries are usually made top-down. They are made by managers. Then the decisions are given to the workers.
Discussion Approach	3)	4)

Words and Expressions

entrepreneurial	/ˌɔːntrəprə'nəːriəl/	*adj.*	企业的，企业家的
entrepreneur	/ˌɔːntrəprə'nəː(r)/	*n.*	企业家
chip	/tʃip/	*n.*	薄片
cookie	/'kuki/	*n.*	小甜饼
Microsoft Corporation	微软公司，创办人是 Bill Gates		
Federal Express	联邦快运公司，创办人是 Frederick Smith		
Mrs. Fields Cookies	菲尔兹食品连锁店，创办人是Bedd Fields		

1. Listen to the passage and fill in the blanks with the information you hear.

1) Bill Gates became famous when he invented ______________________ called MS-DOS. Today he is ______________________ in US.

2) Federal Express , the company that ______________________ anywhere in the United States ______________________, was started ______________________ by a man named Frederick Smith. He was ______________________ at the time. He had first suggested the ideas for his company ______________________. Today his company is worth about ______________________ and employs ______________________.

3) Bedd Fields was ______________________ when she started her first chocolate chip cookie shop at ______________________. There are now ______________________ Mrs. Fields Cookie shops ______________________.

2. Listen to the passage again and write down the reasons why the three entrepreneurs are regarded as heroes.

1) ______________________________

2) ______________________________

3) ______________________________

4) ______________________________

3. Questions for discussion.

1) What are the main factors in the success of the above people?

2) What are your hopes for the future?

Unit Four **Arts**

Part One
Short Conversations

Listen to the following short conversations and choose the best answer to each question you hear.

1. A. Arrange a place for him to study.   B. Help him with some heavy work.
   C. Go away for the weekend.   D. Give him a spare room.
2. A. The train is crowded.   B. The train is late.
   C. The train is empty.   D. The train is on time.
3. A. She can use his car.   B. she can borrow someone else's car.
   C. She must get her car fixed.   D. She can't borrow his car.
4. A. At a cigarette store.   B. At a bus station.
   C. At a gas station.   D. At aunt Mary's.
5. A. A railway porter.   B. A taxi driver.
   C. A bus conductor.   D. A postal clerk.
6. A. It is difficult to identify.   B. It has been misplaced.
   C. It is missing.   D. It has been borrowed by someone.
7. A. She wants to eat out.   B. She wants to fix the mess at home.
   C. She wants to stay at home.   D. She wants to have supper at home.

8. A. He is a good father.
   B. He was once a naughty boy himself.
   C. He has some experience in dealing with boys.
   D. He has several sons.
9. A. She agrees with him partially.
   B. She doesn't agree with him.
   C. She advises him to be more careful.
   D. She suggests that he be strict with his son.
10. A. She doesn't want to ask Jimmy herself.
    B. She doesn't know what to do.
    C. Jimmy might be able to fix the radio.
    D. Jimmy knows who can fix the radio.
11. A. A dentist. B. A teacher.
    C. A cook. D. A tailor.
12. A. At the airport. B. At the hotel.
    C. In the stationery store. D. In the living room.
13. A. It fell out of the camera.
    B. Susan took it to be developed.
    C. Mary developed it in photography class.
    D. The man gave it to Susan.
14. A. He will go to the library. B. He will give the woman a ride.
    C. He will give Jean a ride. D. He will meet Jean.
15. A. Student and teacher. B. Client and lawyer.
    C. Secretary and boss. D. Patient and doctor.

Part Two Dialogue

Have You Ever Heard of the Mona Lisa?

Words and Expressions

authentic	/ɔː'θentik/	*adj.*	真的；真正的
fake	/feik/	*adj.*	假的；伪造的；冒充的
Holland	/'hɔlənd/	*n.*	荷兰

vice versa	反之亦然
Mona Lisa	蒙娜丽莎(达·芬奇所画之著名的画像)
Leonardo da Vinci	达·芬奇
Rembrandt	伦勃朗(荷兰画家)

1. Listen to the dialogue and answer the following questions.

1) Who painted the Mona Lisa?

2) Who was Rembrandt?

3) What are the two kinds of people purchasing paintings according to the dialogue?

4) What does the man want to learn according to the dialogue?

2. Listen to the dialogue again and fill in the blanks with the information you hear.

Woman: Have you ever seen a Rembrandt painting?

Man: Art is so 1) ____________. It is becoming very difficult to separate the difference between 2) ____________ and a fake one. Who's Rembrandt again?

Woman: He's 3) ____________ from Holland who did his most important work in the 1600s.

Man: I have a hard time remembering all of the great artists, 4) ____________.

Woman: Most people have the same problem. Art is one of those 5) ____________.

Man: Yes, I agree. There are two kinds of people. The first, collectors, are 6) ____________ in all the different pieces and their details. The second, investors, have the extra money to purchase art for 7) ____________.

Woman: I'm still just an admirer of good art.

Man: I'd like to learn how to paint abstract art. That would be cool!

Woman: Just paint yourself. That should be 8) ____________.

3. Questions for discussion.

1) Why would a man paint himself as a woman, or vice versa?

2) Do you think investing in art broadens your mind and relaxes your soul?

Part Three Compound Dictation

Silk-screening

Listen to the passage and fill in the blanks with the information you hear.

Silk-screening is the art of producing pictures by printing on specially prepared silk screens. After a thin piece of silk has been tacked (缝) onto a special 1) ________, the picture is cut through the silk by brushing in a layer of 2) ________ that weaken certain areas of the silk. A series of 3) ________ needs to be made for each different layer of color that will be 4) ________ in the final product. It is possible to use 5) ________ colors on one screen, but if you desire 6) ________, clean lines, it is best to use one color per screen.

When the screens have been cut, it is important that some method be used to keep them in an 7) ________ position. If one of the screens is out of place, the printing won't look right. 8) ____. The first screen is applied, and the color is scraped (刮，擦) across the screen with a smooth piece of wood or rubber. This process is known as "pulling". 9) ____. The parts which were cut by the chemicals allow the ink to pass through and create the image. 10) ____.

Part Four Passages

A. The Shaker Furniture

Words and Expressions

persecution	/ˌpəːsi'kjuːʃ(ə)n/	*n.*	迫害
prosper	/'prɔspə/	*v.*	兴隆，昌盛
elaborate	/i'læbərət/	*adj.*	精心制作的
durable	/'djuərəbl/	*adj.*	耐用的；持久的

1. Listen to the passage and choose the best answer to each of the following questions.

1) What is the main subject of this passage?

A. The Shaker religion.

B. The Shaker craftsmanship.

C. The Shaker history.

D. The Shaker museums.

2) In what period did the Shakers thrive?

A. Between 1800 and 1850.

B. From 1850 to 1900.

C. Between 1900 and 1950.

D. Between 1950 to the present.

3) What do people today like about the Shaker furniture?

A. Its decoration. B. Its heaviness.

C. Its design. D. Its cost.

4) How many Shakers are alive today?

A. Six. B. Twelve.

C. Nineteen. D. Twenty.

2. List the characteristics of the Shaker furniture made in the nineteenth century.

1) ________________

2) ________________

3) ________________

4) ________________

5) ________________

B. Trafalgar Square

Words and Expressions

commemorate	/kə'meməreit/	*vt.*	纪念
naval	/'neivəl/	*adj.*	海军的
sculpt	/skʌlpt/	*v.*	雕刻；造型
duke	/djuːk/	*n.*	公爵
rally	/'ræli/	*n.*	聚集；集会
hollow	/'hɔləu/	*adj.*	空的；中空的

1. Listen to the passage and decide whether the following statements are true (T) or false (F).

( ) 1) The Column in Trafalgar Square was built to honor Nelson's victory against the Spanish and French navies.

( ) 2) The statue of Nelson sculpted by Bailey is 5.3 meters high.

( ) 3) Tourists are not allowed to feed pigeons in Trafalgar Square.

( ) 4) The police station in the square is only big enough for a policeman.

( ) 5) Women don't work in the police station in Trafalgar Square.

2. Listen to the passage again and fill in the blanks with the information you hear.

1) The unknown letter writer suggested that the square was ________ to honor Nelson's victory against ________.

2) People also criticized ________, which they said spoilt the Whitehall view.

3) The Duke of York died with debts of ______ and so it was suggested that he should be ______.

4) In Trafalgar Square today, many tourists ______ and British people gather there for ______.

5) They have ______ with New Scotland Yard near Victoria Station and quietly keep an eye on Trafalgar Square when it is ______.

3. Talk with your partner and give details about Trafalgar Square, using the following clue.

1) The unknown letter writer.

2) The designer of Nelson's column and the sculptor of Nelson's statue.

3) The height of the column and the statue.

4) The criticism of Nelson's column.

Unit Five Man and Nature

Part One
Short Conversations

Listen to the following short conversations and choose the best answer to each question you hear.

1. A. His uncle is hard to please. B. His uncle often gets angry.
   C. His uncle often complains. D. His uncle is not always happy.
2. A. It's difficult to give up smoking. B. It's easy to give up smoking.
   C. He doesn't need the woman's advice. D. He thanks the woman for her advice.
3. A. Ann will come in time for the show. B. Ann will surely come.
   C. Ann doesn't want to come. D. Ann will come on time.
4. A. Both speakers think half the staff are efficient.
   B. The woman has a favorable opinion of the staff, but the man does not.
   C. Neither of them has a favorable opinion of the staff.
   D. The man is a restaurant manager himself.
5. A. The question wasn't very clear.
   B. He can have the car if he likes.
   C. He'd better ask someone else.
   D. She can't lend him the car.

6. A. She's not sure where it has been put.
   B. It has been changed recently.
   C. She believes that the number has not been listed.
   D. It can be found in the telephone book.
7. A. Jane walked home.
   B. Jane was not caught in the rain.
   C. Jane was caught in the rain.
   D. It was raining when Jane came back on foot.
8. A. He prefers taking a plane.
   B. He prefers taking a coach.
   C. He prefers travelling with the woman.
   D. He prefers staying at home.
9. A. He thinks that Jane will stay.
   B. He thinks that Jane will feel sorry to leave.
   C. He thinks that Jane will buy him a present.
   D. He thinks that Jane will go away.
10. A. They should definitely do it.
    B. They should have done it earlier.
    C. They should try every means to do it.
    D. They should not do it now.
11. A. The woman's credit card is stolen.
    B. The man is very worried because his card will be invalidated soon.
    C. The man is in trouble.
    D. The man is anxious to know if he can get a new card.
12. A. The talks have produced a general agreement.
    B. The talks haven't started yet.
    C. The talks haven't achieved much.
    D. The talks broke down and could go no further.
13. A. The man ate during the show.
    B. Four contestants failed to win prizes.
    C. The woman missed the show.
    D. Five contestants won cars.
14. A. She thinks that schools should improve students' ability to compete in future.
    B. She thinks that a million-dollar-a-year job is better than studying hard at school.
    C. She hopes that her son will be able to get a money-earning job later in life.
    D. She believes that school children shouldn't be given so much pressure.
15. A. The man has it.
    B. The man has thrown the list into the waste paper basket.
    C. It's in a book.
    D. The woman has it.

Part Two Dialogue

What Happens to the Baby Seals?

Words and Expressions

painlessly	/'peinlisli/	*adv.*	不痛地，没有痛苦地
club	/klʌb/	*n.*	棍棒
		vt.	用棍棒打
chase	/tʃeis/	*vt.*	追逐
petition	/pi'tiʃən/	*n.*	请愿；请愿书；诉状
donation	/dəu'neiʃ(ə)n/	*n.*	捐赠；捐款
Disneyland	/'dizni,lænd/	*n.*	迪斯尼乐园
Friends of the Earth			"地球的朋友"(一动物保护组织)

1. Listen to the dialogue and choose the right answers to the following questions.

1) What did the woman intend to do?

A. To buy fur coats.

B. To boycott the fur store.

2) How were the baby seals killed?

A. To be clubbed to death. | B. To be cut by the throat.

3) What did the man ask the woman to do for "Friends of the Earth"?

A. To sign the petition. | B. To give a donation.

4) What would the woman do next?

A. To go to the sales. | B. To refuse to buy anything from the store.

2. Listen to the dialogue again and fill in the blanks with the information you hear.

Man: Madam, can I have a word with you?

Woman: Well ... er ... I'm 1) ______________________. I'm going to the sales of the fur coats.

Man: It won't take a moment.

Woman: OK.

Man: Do you know why we're 2) ______________________ outside this store?

Woman: Oh, it's something to do with the fur coats, isn't it? They've got some 3) ______________________.

Man: Do you know how many animals are killed to make one coat? Do you know what happens to baby seals 4) ______________________?

Woman: Well, they're put to death painlessly, aren't they?

Man: They're clubbed to death. 5) ______________________. They're taken from their mothers, chased across the ice, and then beaten to death with clubs.

Woman: They have to be controlled. If they aren't controlled, they eat 6) ______________________. They have to be killed.

Man: They don't have to be killed, you know. It's only 7) ______________________ that says that. Nature has its own way of control. Look at the picture of that poor little seal. It's all 8) ______________________.

Woman: Oh, it's horrible!

Man: That's how the seals are killed. That's the evidence.

***Woman*:** Here I'll 9) ________________.

***Man*:** Perhaps you'd like to 10) ________________ to "Friends of the Earth"? You can stop the world's wildlife from disappearing.

***Woman*:** Yes. I think I will. But I'd still like to 11) ________________.

***Man*:** One day there won't be any wild animals left in the world. You'll just have 12) ________________ in Disneyland.

3. Questions for discussion.

1) Have you ever seen seals? How much do you know about them?
2) Would you work out any effective ways of dissuading people from purchasing fur coats?

Part Three Compound Dictation

The Balance of Nature

Listen to the passage and fill in the blanks with the information you hear.

It is only during the last few years that man has become generally aware that in the world of nature a most delicate balance exists between all forms of life. No living things can 1) ________________ by itself: it is part of a system in which all forms of life are 2) ________________ together. If we change one part of the 3) ________________ order, this will in its turn almost 4) ________________ bring about changes in some other part.

The cutting down of 5) __________ reduces the supply of oxygen. The killing of weeds and 6) __________ by chemicals leads to the 7) __________ poisoning of animals and birds. 8) __________ __________, while exhaust fumes change the chemical balance of the atmosphere and shut out some of the sun's essential life-giving rays.

And so we could go on, adding more examples, until in despair we might feel like giving up the struggle to control and keep within limits these harmful human activities. 9) __________, but he is not so clever at looking far ahead, or at thinking about what the future results of his actions might be. 10) __________.

Part Four Passages

A. Outdoor Plants Move Inside

Words and Expressions

indoors	/ˌin'dɔːz/	*adv.*	在户内，室内
orchid	/'ɔːkid/	*n.*	[植]兰花
tropical	/'trɔpik(ə)l/	*adj.*	热带的；热带性的
thrive	/θraiv/	*v.*	茁壮成长；旺盛

exotic	/ig'zɔtik/	*adj.*	异国情调的；外来的；奇异的
vine	/vain/	*n.*	葡萄树；蔓生植物；攀缘植物
parasitic	/ˌpærə'sitik/	*adj.*	寄生的
redwood	/'redwud/	*n.*	[植]红杉

1. Listen to the passage and choose the best answer to each of the following questions.

1) What did people previously believe about plants indoors?

A. The plants that could grow indoors were limited.

B. The climate was killing the plants.

C. The climate was in danger.

D. The larger plants grew better inside.

2) What do modern windows do?

A. Allow fresh air in.

B. Keep out the insects.

C. Provide warmth and light.

D. Control the temperature.

3) Why is it unlikely that large plants will move indoors?

A. The climate is not suitable.

B. They cannot be moved.

C. They cannot be controlled.

D. There is not enough space indoors.

4) What is the main point of the talk?

A. The global warming problem.

B. The difficulty of controlling the climate.

C. Growing plants indoors.

D. Endangered plants.

2. Listen to the passage again and write down the information according to what you have heard.

1) The reasons why many outdoor plants have moved inside.

a. ____

____

b. ____

____

2) List the plants which thrive in indoor surroundings.

a. ____

____

b. ____

____

B. World's Rivers Running Dry

Words and Expressions

divert	/dai'vəːt/	*v.*	转移；转向
lettuce	/'letis/	*n.*	[植]莴苣；生菜
bathtub	/'bɑːθtʌb/	*n.*	浴缸；澡盆
turbine	/'təːbin, -bain/	*n.*	涡轮
diversion	/dai'vəːʃən/	*n.*	转移；转换
majestic	/mə'dʒestik/	*adj.*	雄伟的，壮丽的
torrent	/'tɔrənt/	*n.*	急流；洪流
trickle	/'trik(ə)l/	*n.*	细流；滴
quench	/kwentʃ/	*vt.*	熄灭；解渴
irrigation	/ˌiri'geiʃən/	*n.*	灌溉；冲洗
incentive	/in'sentiv/	*n.*	动机

siphon	/'saifən/	*vt.*	用虹吸管吸；外流；消耗
Arizona	/ˌæri'zəunə/	*n.*	亚利桑那州(美国)
Jordan River			约旦河
Salt and Gila Rivers			盐河和西拉河(美国)
drip irrigation lines			滴流灌溉线
low-pressure sprinklers			低压喷洒装置

1. Listen to the passage and decide whether the following statements are true (T) or false (F).

( ) 1) People divert big rivers of the world mainly for agricultural and industrial purpose.

( ) 2) The ecology and habitat for wildlife will be greatly affected if man stops diverting the rivers to meet his needs.

( ) 3) The growing population and its increasing need for water lead to the drying of many rivers.

( ) 4) In the past 50 years, man's demand for water has at least tripled.

( ) 5) Drip irrigation lines or low-pressure sprinklers are ways to save water.

2. Listen to the passage again and fill in the blanks with the information you hear.

1) Of the world's total water demand, about ____________ is for agriculture and another ____________ goes for industrial use. The ____________ remaining quenches thirsts in cities and towns.

2) In an effort to tame and use the rivers' flow, governments began ____________. There were ____________ large dams in 1950. There are ____________

_________ today.

3) The demand for water has _____________

_____________.

3. What do you think of the river(s) in the city where you live? Has the local government done anything to preserve the river?

Unit Six Social Welfare

Part One Short Conversations

Listen to the following short conversations and choose the best answer to each question you hear.

1. A. They will buy a new car instead of going on a holiday.
   B. They will go on a holiday instead of buying a new car.
   C. They will buy a smaller house and a new car.
   D. They will not buy a new car because they don't have enough money left now.
2. A. The man will go home during the spring holiday.
   B. The man will graduate before spring holiday.
   C. The man will not graduate in May.
   D. The man will not go home during the spring holiday.
3. A. A salesman. B. A student. C. A tailor. D. A customer.
4. A. John will not be able to sell his house.
   B. John was joking.
   C. John is probably serious with his decision.
   D. He agrees with the woman.

5. A. Mrs. Smith felt bored when the man asked.
   B. The man was so sorry for Mrs. Smith's problems.
   C. Mrs. Smith was so busy that she could not help the man.
   D. Mrs. Smith was willing to help her neighbor.
6. A. The birds are very pretty.
   B. The birds are very expensive.
   C. They couldn't possibly afford the birds.
   D. Both B and C.
7. A. They are holding a dancing party.
   B. They are planning a surprise party.
   C. They are having a meeting.
   D. They are making an appointment.
8. A. The woman's husband. B. A doctor.
   C. A plumber. D. A policeman.
9. A. Tony won't lend her any money.
   B. Tony always keeps his promise.
   C. Tony is very mean with his money.
   D. Tony will buy a house for himself.
10. A. On Wednesday. B. On Thursday. C. On Friday. D. On Tuesday.
11. A. It is an optimistic one.
    B. It varies according to her mood.
    C. It is usually sarcastic.
    D. It is determined by what she reads in the newspapers.
12. A. She believes she can do very well. B. She is not prepared.
    C. The examination is unfair. D. She has no confidence.
13. A. It is his mother who told him to become a teacher.
    B. It is his father who told him to become a good manager.
    C. His teacher told him to get his teaching degree.
    D. "Try to be a teacher and your life will be assured," his father said.
14. A. It's unnecessary to copy all the questions.
    B. Questions are easy on the exam paper.
    C. These questions are all nonsense.
    D. They don't like talking about women.
15. A. The woman would understand why Frank is always complaining if she had Frank's job.
    B. Frank could help her get a job on an airplane.
    C. Waiting on tables is an enjoyable job.
    D. He is tired to waiting for her there.

Part Two Dialogue

Is the United States A Welfare State?

Words and Expressions

social stratification			社会阶层
access to rewards			获取报酬
municipal clinics and hospitals			市立诊所和市立医院
Blue Cross			(美国)蓝十字会(一种健康保险组织)
Blue Shield			(美国)蓝盾(一种健康保险政策)
Medicare	/'medi,kɛə/	n.	(美国、加拿大)老年保健医疗(制度)
Medicaid	/'medikeid/	n.	(美国)医疗补助(制度)

1. Listen to the dialogue and choose the best answer to complete the following sentences.

1) The key reason why the United States isn't a welfare state is that ________.

A. it doesn't have a health-care system

B. it doesn't have a national health-insurance program

C. the rich Americans don't care about a welfare system

D. medical care is regarded as a private business

2) The richest fifth of American individuals and families own over __________ of the wealth.

A. 25%　　B. 35%　　C. 75%　　D. 98%

3) "The poor have to attend municipal clinics and hospitals" implies __________.

A. there are not-for-profit medical institutions

B. the rich can enjoy medical treatment at home

C. only the rich can afford to attend expensive private hospitals

D. a kind of concern for the poor on the part of the city government

4) __________ is designed to cover doctors' fees for medical and surgical expenses.

A. Blue Cross　　B. Blue Shield　　C. Medicare　　D. Medicaid

5) We can infer that the " Blues" as well as Medicare and Medicaid programs are designed to __________.

A. protect the benefits of doctors and hospitals

B. help the poor and the old so that they may receive timely and due medical treatment

C. ensure that the poor and the old sharc some of the social welfare

D. tell that the United States is on its way to a welfare state

2. Listen to the dialogue again and then explain the following in English.

1) social stratification

____

2) Blue Cross

____

3) Blue Shield

____

4) Medicare

____

5) Medicaid

____

3. Questions for discussion.

1) Suppose you live in the United States, do you think it important to buy medical insurance for yourself?

2) Suppose you are a rich American, would you prefer to attend an expensive private hospital or a municipal one?

3) Talk about the US welfare spending with your partner according to the following chart.

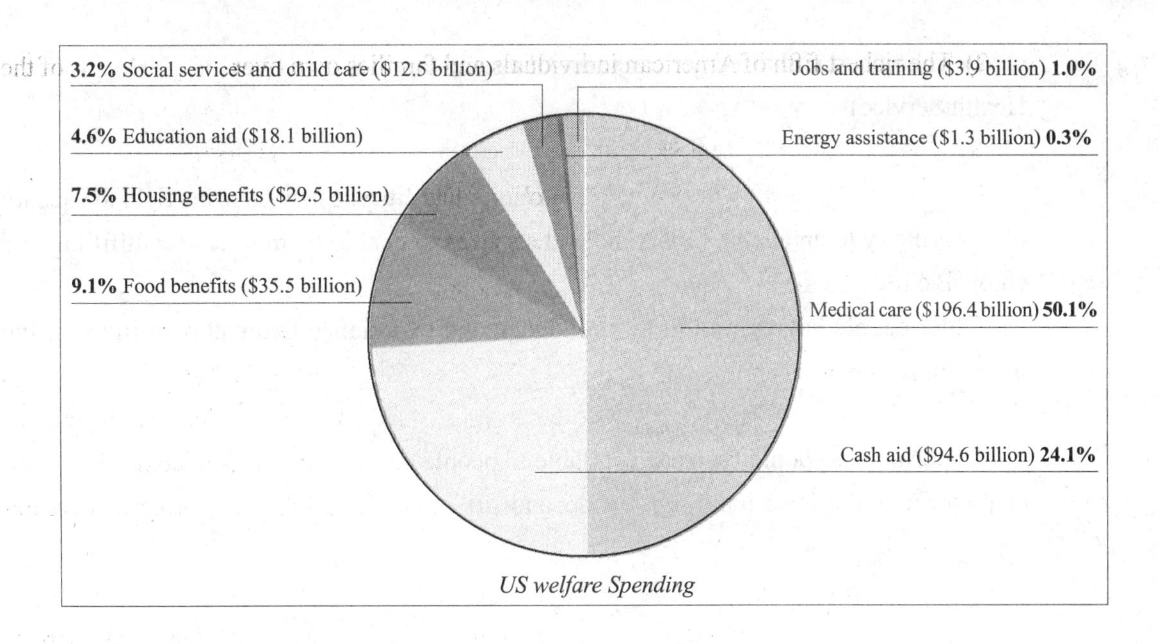

US welfare Spending

Part Three Compound Dictation

Old People in Britain

Listen to the passage and fill in the blanks with the information you hear.

According to the British government figures, more than half of the nation's single pensioners have net incomes of less than £90 a week. A 1) ______________ of couples have net incomes of less than £135 a week. While to achieve an "acceptable" standard of living for older people and to avoid 2) ______________, the figures, according to a research commissioned by Age Concern England, 3) ______________ from £99 to £125 a week for single people and from £149 to £184 for couples.

Coupled with low net incomes is the health needs of older people. The health needs of older people cannot be 4) ______________ from their level of income and housing conditions. If older people are poor, ill-housed and 5) ______________ excluded, they are more likely to become physically and 6) ______________ ill. In addition, recent research undertaken by Age

Concern England identified the existence of age 7) ________ within NHS (National Health Service).

8) ____. As individual citizens they have the right to equality of opportunity to an adequate income and services to enable them to lead a fulfilling and enjoyable life.

Older people have a wealth of knowledge and experience that can be utilized to the benefit of society as a whole. 9) ____.

Opportunities should be made available to people aged 50 and over to continue in paid employment if this is what they wish to do; and 10) ____.

Part Four Passages

A. Why is Britain Dubbed as A Welfare State?

Words and Expressions

dub	/dʌb/	*v.*	把……称为
supplementary	/ˌsʌpli'ment(ə)ri/	*adj.*	增补的，补充的
supplementary benefits	补助费；补助救济金		
the welfare state	福利国家		
National Insurance	(英国)国民保险制度(失业养老保险制度)		
National Health (Service)	(英国)国民保险制度(免费医疗制度)		

1. Listen to the passage and choose the best answer to complete the following sentences.

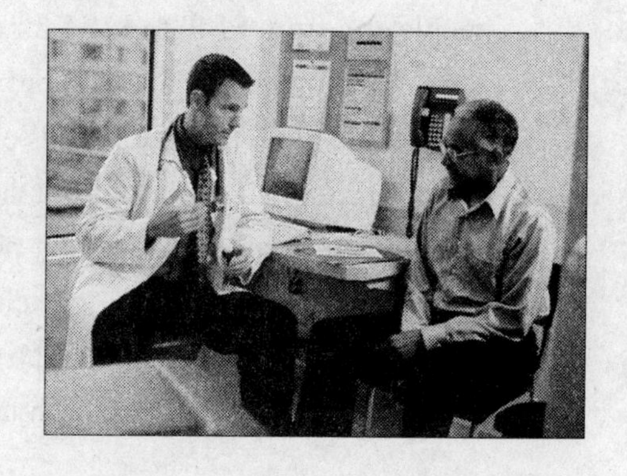

1) ________ is the most important under the social state system.

A. The guarantee of the means of the minimum necessities of life

B. The National Insurance System

C. The National Health Service

D. Supplementary profits

2) Under National Health Service, all are free except ________.

A. doctors' services

B. services from specialists

C. staying in hospital

D. a small charge (£5) for medicine

3) The reason for some people who are entitled to benefits to still live in poverty is that they are too ________.

A. stupid

B. proud

C. confused

D. neglected

2. Listen to the passage again and answer the following questions.

1) To what welfare schemes must an employed British citizen contribute?

____

2) Who else must also contribute?

____

3) Who makes the greatest contributions to the National Health Service?

____

____

4) When was the National Insurance and Health Schemes reorganized?

____

____

B. A Generous Gift

Words and Expressions

charity	/'tʃæriti/	*n.*	慈善事业；慈善机构
in the disadvantage			处于劣势

public welfare project	公共福利事业
benefit performance	义演
collecting box	募捐箱

1. Listen to the passage and choose the best answer to each of the following questions.

1) Who was the woman collecting money for?

A. Poor children. B. A church.

C. Poor people. D. Poor parents.

2) How much money did most people give the woman?

A. A lot of money. B. A few dollars.

C. A few coins. D. From a few coins to $100.

3) Why didn't the artist give money to the woman?

A. Because he was not a generous man.

B. Because he had too many paintings.

C. Because his paintings were worth a lot of money.

D. Because he had no money with him.

4) How did the artist help the woman to get another $100?

A. By giving her the required amount.

B. By giving her another painting which is just worth $100.

C. By telling her to add $100 to the value of his painting.

D. By changing the original painting with another one.

2. Listen to the passage again and fill in the blanks with the information you hear.

1) Actors and actresses ________________ often give benefit performances to ________________ for the poor and needy.

2) Those who are ________________ but with any performing skills and with a kind heart, also take part by offering to ________________.

3) A woman was ________________ for a church charity. Most of the people she called on gave her very little money, but an artist ________________ instead. When she asked him again to give to the charity, he ________________ of the painting.

3. If you see someone hold out a collecting box, will you put some money in it? Why or why not?

Unit Seven **Distance Learning**

Part One Short Conversations

Listen to the following short conversations and choose the best answer to each question you hear.

1. A. She thinks Tom is a poor dancer.
   B. She thinks Tom is a good dancer.
   C. She is fed up with the food served by Tom.
   D. She is tired of dancing all night with him.
2. A. The woman wants to go to the cash-desk.
   B. The woman wants to go to the food counter.
   C. The woman wants to go to the main entrance.
   D. The woman wants to go to the checkroom.
3. A. In an office. B. In a laundry.
   C. In a clothing store. D. In a second-hand clothing store.
4. A. The modern art. B. The classical art.
   C. Both modern and classical art. D. Neither.
5. A. Miss Green. B. John.
   C. Austen. D. All of them.

6. A. Tea. B. Wine. C. Soda water. D. Coffee.
7. A. Husband and wife. B. Teacher and student.
   C. Salesman and customer. D. Doctor and patient.
8. A. Because he loves games.
   B. Because he will watch them on television.
   C. Because he is a sportsman.
   D. Because the last games were far from satisfactory.
9. A. Something happened to her car.
   B. She wanted to visit some shops.
   C. She got up too late to catch the bus.
   D. Her car was separated into parts in the driveway.
10. A. Motorcycles in other shops are inexpensive.
    B. This motorcycle is expensive.
    C. Motorcycles in this shop are very cheap.
    D. Motorcycles' price in this shop is reasonable.
11. A. 8:15 a.m. B. 8:50 p.m. C. 8:50 a.m. D. 8:15 p.m.
12. A. The sales of industrial products are seven times that before liberation.
    B. The sales of industrial products are eight times that before liberation.
    C. The sales of industrial products are six times that before liberation.
    D. The sales of industrial products are nine times as many as that before liberation.
13. A. 38042. B. 388042. C. 3888042. D. 8880042.
14. A. 13. B. 65. C. 78. D. 52.
15. A. 45 minutes. B. 30 minutes. C. 15 minutes. D. 55 minutes.

Part Two Dialogue

I Will Try It Out

Words and Expressions

registration	/ˌredʒisˈtreiʃ(ə)n/	*n.*	登记；注册
impersonal	/imˈpəːsənl/	*adj.*	冷淡的
sail right			轻快地走过
sign up			报名
catch on			流行

1. Listen to the dialogue and choose the best answer to each of the following questions.

1) Where did Mike see the woman yesterday?

A. On television. B. At registration.

C. In class. D. At work.

2) How was the distance learning course different from traditional courses?

A. It's non-traditional and very popular.

B. It's open to everyone who wants to sign up for it.

C. Students taking this course have to do a lot of experiments.

D. It may help a lot with the students' schedules and facilitate their learning.

3) What can we know about distance learning according to the passage?

A. Students are not required to attend regular class lectures.

B. The professor videotapes class lectures for review.

C. Professors are to meet students in various locations throughout the area.

D. Students receive credit for work experience.

4) Why did Linda decide to enroll in the distance learning course?

A. It's a requirement for psychology majors.

B. She wasn't able to get into the traditional course.

C. She lives far from the university.

D. She has to work a lot of hours this semester.

5) What does Linda mean at the end of the conversation?

A. She is sure that she will like distance learning.

B. She is sure that she will hate distance learning.

C. She is not sure whether the course will be good or not.

D. She likes experiment.

2. Listen to the dialogue again and answer the following questions.

1) What's the major advantage of distance learning?

2) What's the disadvantage of distance learning?

3) What are the remedies for the disadvantage?

3. Make sentences with the following idioms.

1) sign up

2) catch on

3) make sense

Part Three Compound Dictation

Distance Education in Britain

Listen to the passage and fill in the blanks with the information you hear.

Distance education refers to methods of instruction that utilize different communications technologies to carry teaching to learners in different places. Distance education programs enable learners and teachers to 1) ______________ with each other by means of computers, 2) ____________ satellites, telephones, radio or television broadcasting, or other technologies. Instruction conducted through the mail is often referred to as 3) ____________ education, although many educators simply consider this the ancestor of distance education. Distance education is also sometimes called distance learning. While distance learning can refer to either formal or informal learning experiences, distance education refers 4) ____________ to formal instruction conducted at a distance by a teacher who plans, guides, and 5) ____________ the learning process. As new communications technologies become more 6) ____________ and more widely 7) ____________, increasing numbers of elementary schools, secondary schools, universities, and businesses offer distance education programs.

In Britain, from elementary schools to graduate schools, people have always focused much of their attention on formal education. At the same time, however, they have always maintained informal channels for learning well into adulthood, whether in the form of Bible classes, library programs, museum exhibitions, or other group activities. 8) ____________
____.

Britain's nationally supported Open University, based in Milton Keynes, Buckinghamshire (白金汉郡), England, has one of the best-known programs. A vast majority of the school's 133,000 students receive instruction entirely at a distance. 9) ____________________

____.

This method of education can be especially valuable in developing countries. By reaching a large number of students with relatively few teachers, it provides a cost-effective way of using limited academic resources. 10) ____________________

____

____.

Part Four Passages

A. History of Distance Education

Words and Expressions

disability	/ˌdisə'biliti/	*n.*	残疾
enroll	/in'rəul/	*v.*	登记；招收
teleconference	/ˌteli'kɔnfərəns/	*n.*	远程电信会议
simultaneously	/ˌsim(ə)l'teiniəsli/	*adv.*	同时
in real time			实时地
gain access to			得以使用

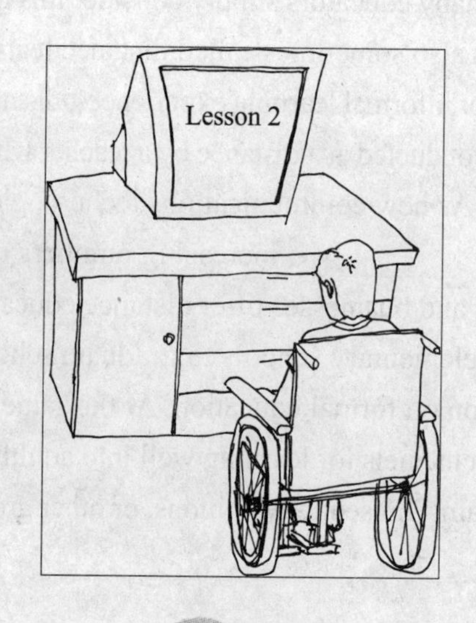

1. Listen to the passage and decide whether the following statements are true (T) or false (F).

( ) 1) People first used television as the media of distance education.

( ) 2) Those who most benefited from early distance education included disabled people.

( ) 3) The invention of radio did not influence distance education as much as television.

( ) 4) Conventional teaching institutions got rid of their walls in the 1940s.

( ) 5) Telephone systems never play a prominent role in education.

( ) 6) Television pictures can be transmitted in two directions simultaneously through telephone lines.

( ) 7) Video-conferencing increases the interaction between students in different places.

2. Listen to the passage again and complete the following chart.

When	What New Media Used in Distance Education
mid-19th century	
in the 1920s	
in the 1940s	
in the early 1900s	
in the 1980s and 1990s	
in the 1980s and 1990s	

B. IT and Language Learning

Words and Expressions

multimedia	/'mʌlti'miːdjə/	*n.*	多媒体
ponderous	/'pɔndərəs/	*adj.*	冗长的；沉闷的
captivate	/'kæptiveit/	*vt.*	吸引；迷住
computer literate			懂计算机的
opt for			选择
EFL (English as a Foreign Language)			作为外国语的英语

1. Listen to the passage and decide whether the following statements are true (T) or false (F).

( ) 1) Nowadays, the language laboratory is supposed to revolutionize language learning.

( ) 2) Almost every institution in the UK has an IT center.

( ) 3) IT and language learning can work well together.

( ) 4) Students have always been forced to deal with lots of textbooks.

( ) 5) Multimedia can motivate young students easily, but not the older ones.

( ) 6) For older learners the creative potential of CALL can help their study.

( ) 7) Multimedia has grown greatly in many fields except in the area of business.

( ) 8) The use of Internet is the latest innovation in CALL.

2. Listen to the passage again and choose the best answer to each of the following questions.

1) Which of the following can be inferred from the passage?

   A. Students now do not need books any longer.

   B. People get PC software mainly from supermarkets.

   C. IT and language learning have been closely related for a long time.

   D. Not all the IT centers in the UK have good facilities.

2) What can we know about the motivating influence of multimedia from the passage?

   A. Multimedia motivates young learners best.

   B. Multimedia motivates adult learners best.

   C. Multimedia can motivate learners better than the traditional medium.

   D. Multimedia and textbooks are equally motivating.

3) What really helps adult learners with their language acquisition as far as multimedia are concerned?

   A. The creative potential of CALL.

   B. Pictures.

   C. Softwares.

   D. Authentic materials.

4) For what purposes do language learners use Internet?

   A. For language practice, research support and creation of pages on the Net.

   B. For language practice, research support and business transaction.

   C. For language practice, cyber-chat and creation of pages on the Net.

   D. For language practice, business transaction and research support.

3. Questions for discussion.

1) Do you know any correspondence school in China? Do you have any family members who take correspondence courses?

2) What do you think are the technological conditions that make the development of distance learning possible?

3) What are the possible influences of the Internet upon distance learning?

4) Which do you prefer, traditional learning or distance learning? Why? Please summarize the reasons for your preference.

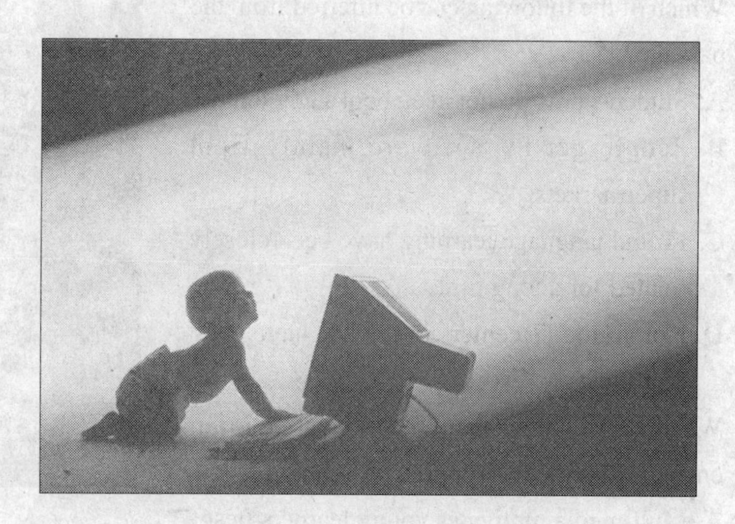

Unit Eight Famous Speeches

Part One Short Conversations

Listen to the following short conversations and choose the best answer to each question you hear.

1. A. It's cooler. B. It's warmer
   C. It's cold. D. It's like his home.
2. A. Living in the country. B. Living in the city.
   C. Living with her parents. D. Living in the place where she was born.
3. A. In a library. B. In a book store.
   C. In a book company. D. In a booking office.
4. A. The man's living condition is very good actually.
   B. The woman's living condition is better than the man's.
   C. The woman's living condition is equally miserable.
   D. Both of them are living in a very good condition.
5. A. The wind has stopped but it's still raining.
   B. The rain has stopped.
   C. It's still raining and the wind is blowing.
   D. Both the rain and the wind have stopped.

6. A. April. B. June. C. May. D. July.
7. A. At 12:15. B. At 1:00. C. At 1:10. D: At 12:30.
8. A. To her native place. B. To his hometown.
C. To the summer resort. D. To the hills.
9. A. A customer. B. A saleswoman. C. A waitress. D. An operator.
10. A. A dentist. B. A teacher. C. A cook. D. A tailor.
11. A. More than one hundred people. B. One thousand people.
C. More than one thousand people. D. One hundred people.
12. A. $125. B. $15. C. $105. D. $140.
13. A. 25 pounds. B. 20 pounds. C. 205 pounds. D. 225 pounds.
14. A. At 11:00. B. At 9:15. C. At 12:50. D. At 10:01.
15. A. Dec. 13th, 1916. B. Nov. 13th, 1906.
C. Dec. 30th, 1906. D. Nov. 13th, 1916.

Part Two Dialogue

Why, Mom, You Are Weeping?

Words and Expressions

thrill	/θril/	*n. & v.*	感到非常兴奋，激动
smuggle	/'smʌgl/	*v.*	私运；走私
opium	/'əupiəm/	*n.*	鸦片
confiscate	/'kɔnfiskeit/	*vt.*	没收
Canton	/kæn'tɔn/	*n.*	广州(旧称)
pretext	/'priːtekst/	*n.*	托辞，借口
cede	/siːd/	*vt.*	割让
artisan	/ˌɑːti'zæn; (*US*) 'ɑːrtizn/	*n.*	工匠

1. Listen to the dialogue and fill in the blanks with the information you hear.

In the 1830s — that's a very long time ago — British merchants began to 1)____________ into China from India. Opium is 2)____________ to human beings. China had banned the opium trade 3)____________. But the British went on poisoning our Chinese. Later, 4)____________ named Lin Zexu confiscated a lot of opium and 5)____________. The British used this as a pretext and 6)____________ against China. Just like the Japanese 7)____________ decades ago. By *the Treaty of Nanking* in 1842, 8)____________.

2. Retell the story about Hong Kong in the voice of 1) Dongdong to other children; 2) a student whose major is Chinese History.

3. Questions for discussion.

1) What do you think about the return of Hong Kong?

2) Use your imagination to draw a picture of Hong Kong's future.

Part Three Compound Dictation

Farewell to Hong Kong

By Prince Charles

Listen to the passage and fill in the blanks with the information you hear.

Governor, Prime Minister, ladies and gentlemen, I've been asked by Her Majesty the Queen to read the following message.

Five hours from now the Union flag will be lowered and the flag of China will fly over Hong Kong. More than a century and a half of British 1) ________________ will come to an end. During that time Hong Kong has grown from a small 2) ________________ settlement into one of the leading cities and one of the greatest trading economies in the world. There have been times of sacrifice, suffering and 3) ________________. As Hong Kong has risen from the ashes of war, a most 4) ________________ transformation has taken place; millions of destitute (穷困的) immigrants have been absorbed and Hong Kong has created one of the most successful 5) ________________ on earth. Britain is both proud and privileged to be involved with this success story. Proud of the British values and institutions that have been the 6) ________________ for Hong Kong's success. Proud of the rights and freedoms which Hong Kong people enjoy. Privileged to be associated with the prodigiously (令人吃惊地) talented and 7) ________________ people of Hong Kong who have built upon that foundation. The British flag will be lowered and British administrative responsibility will end. But Britain is not saying good-bye to Hong Kong. 8) ____. Thousands of young Hong Kong men and women study in Britain every year. We share language and the English Common Law. And thousands of Britains too, have made their homes in Hong Kong. 9) ____.

Britain is part of Hong Kong's history and Hong Kong is part of Britain's history. We are also part of each other's future. 10) ____.

The eyes of the world are on Hong Kong today. I wish you all a successful transition and a prosperous and peaceful future.

Part Four Passages

A. Blood, Toil, Sweat and Tears

By Winston Leonard Spencer Churchill

Words and Expressions

inflexible	/in'fleksib(ə)l/	*adj.*	不可改变的；不屈的
prosecute	/'prɔsikjuːt/	*v.*	进行(战争)
preliminary	/pri'liminəri/	*adj.*	预备的；初步的
ordeal	/ɔː'diːl/	*n.*	折磨
grievous	/'griːvəs/	*adj.*	严重伤害的；引起痛苦的
wage	/weidʒ/	*v.*	发动
monstrous	/'mɔnstrəs/	*adj.*	可怕的

tyranny	/'tirəni/	n.	暴政；专治
lamentable	/'læməntəbl/	adj.	令人惋惜的；悔恨的
buoyancy	/'bɔiənsi/	n.	浮力；(指人、态度等)振作起来，乐天
juncture	/'dʒʌŋktʃə/	n.	时刻；关头
Norway	/'nɔːwei/	n.	挪威
Holland	/'hɔlənd/	n.	荷兰
Mediterranean	/ˌmeditə'reinjən/	n.	地中海
		adj.	地中海(地区)的

Background information:

Churchill, Sir Winston Leonard Spencer, 1874—1965, British statesman, soldier, and author. From 1929 to 1939, Churchill issued unheeded warnings of the threat of Nazi Germany. In 1940, seven months after the outbreak of World War II, he replaced Neville Chamberlain as Prime Minister. His stirring oratory, his energy, and his refusal to make peace with Hitler were crucial to maintaining British resistance from 1940 to 1942. After the postwar Labour victory in 1945, he became leader of the opposition. In 1951 he was again elected Prime Minister; he was knighted in 1953 and retired in 1955. Churchill was the author of many histories, biographies, and memoirs, and in 1953 he was awarded the Nobel Prize in literature for his writing and his oratory.

1. Sentence dictation.

1) ______________________________

____

____

2) ______________________________

3) ______________________________

____

____

2. Listen to the passage and choose the best answer to each of the following questions.

1) What is the aim of the new government?

A. Survival. B. Existence.

C. Victory. D. War.

2) What is the policy of the new government?

A. To wage war by land, sea and air.

B. To wage war against Nazi Germany.

C. To wage war with all might and strength against Hitler.

D. All of the above.

3) Who is the leader of the new government?

A. His Majesty.

B. Winston Leonard Spencer Churchill.

C. Ministers.

D. Opposition.

4) What's Churchill's aim in the address?

A. To offer his blood, toil, tears and sweat.

B. To ask the House to pardon him.

C. To call on the British people to go forward together with united strength.

D. To take up his task as Prime Minister.

5) Which of the following statements is TRUE?

A. To form an administration of this scale and complexity is a serious piece of work itself.

B. The British army has taken action in Norway, Holland and the Mediterranean.

C. The whole nation welcomes the formation of the new Parliament.

D. It's a long way to success without Churchill's blood, toil, tears and sweat.

D-Day Troops in World War II

3. **Talk about the chief events in the life of Winston Churchill and make comments on his contribution to Great Britain and the victory of World War II.**

B. Commencement Address at Harvard University

by Mary Robinson on June 4, 1998

Words and Expressions

commencement	/kə'mensmənt/	*n.*	大学的毕业典礼
rigor	/'rigə(r)/	*n.*	严格；严厉
assume	/ə'sjuːm/	*vt.*	承担(任务)；掌握(权力)
soundness	/'saundnis/	*n.*	完善；健全
beneficiary	/ˌbeni'fiʃəri/	*n.*	领受人，受益人
exceptional	/ik'sepʃənl/	*adj.*	特殊的
innately	/i'neitli/	*adv.*	生来地，天生地
rejuvenate	/ri'dʒuːvineit/	*v.*	使恢复青春，充满活力
Harvard	/'hɑːvəd/	*n.*	哈佛大学(美国)
embark on			从事，着手，开始
be answerable to			对……负责

Background information:

Mary Robinson was born on 21 May, 1944. She was inaugurated as the seventh President of Ireland in 1990 and resigned from the office of President in 1997, to take up appointment as United Nations High Commissioner for Human Rights.

1. Listen to the passage and choose the best answer to each of the following questions.

1) To whom is the speaker giving the address?

A. The graduating class of 1998.
B. The students' families and friends.
C. The president of Harvard University.
D. All of the above.

2) What can we learn about the speaker from the passage?

A. She graduated from Harvard in 1968.
B. She is going to graduate from Harvard in 1998.
C. Her father graduated from Harvard in 1968.
D. Her daughter is going to graduate from Harvard in 1998.

3) What kind of world will the graduates face?

A. A world full of possibilities.
B. A world full of possibilities but not for all.
C. A world full of responsibilities.
D. A world full of responsibilities but not for all.

4) Which of the following statements is TRUE?

A. The speaker is proud because she will put years of learning and preparation to good use.
B. The graduates are proud because they have passed through the rigors of a formal education.
C. The graduates have received an exceptional education at an exceptional place.
D. The graduates feel guilty because they have received an exceptional education at an exceptional place.

5) Which of the following statements is NOT true?

A. The graduates should be proud of what they have achieved.
B. According to the speaker, the graduates become answerable only to themselves with regard to their performance, humanity and soundness of judgment.
C. The graduates are not encouraged because they will use their education to pursue only the worthiest of goals.
D. According to the speaker, the graduates should contribute to the betterment of the lives of others.

2. Use the following words and phrases as clues to make out the main contents of the address.

assume	be answerable to	commencement	goal
embark on	exceptional	congratulations	graduate
possibility	Harvard University	preparation	promise
rejuvenate	put ... to good use	responsibility	rigors

3. Questions for discussion.

1) What do you think a recent graduate should do in a world full of possibilities?
2) What do you want to do after graduation?
3) According to the speaker, the graduates of Harvard University have received an exceptional education at an exceptional place. What do you think about her opinion?

Commencement Congratulations

Unit Nine Economic Development

Part One Short Conversations

ng short conversations and choose the best answer to each

B. 20. C. 25. D. 30.

y. B. At an airport.

D. At a bus stop.

3. rt books from the library.

B. She should buy some good art books.

C. She can borrow his books on art.

D. She shouldn't be so interested in art.

4. A. He learned Spanish very well in Spain.

B. He has made no progress in Spanish.

C. He doesn't like speaking Spanish.

D. He has just begun to learn Spanish.

5. A. She bought nothing.

B. She caught a cold.

C. She bought some medicine.

D. She became sick and didn't go shopping.

6. A. It's wonderful. B. It's not well-made.
   C. It's out of fashion. D. It's unfit.
7. A. Peter always helps Ruth. B. Peter made a mistake in helping Ruth.
   C. Ruth wants to marry Peter. D. Ruth decides not to marry Peter.
8. A. She bought them at the theatre. B. She bought them from the director.
   C. She was given them by the director. D. She got them from a friend of the director.
9. A. Paint the bookshelf. B. Fix the table.
   C. Wash the car. D. Go to the beach.
10. A. She is an engineer. B. She is a mathematician.
    C. She is the manager of a company. D. She is an artist.
11. A. Watch something on TV. B. Go for a ride in a car.
    C. Read the newspaper. D. Leave for the airport.
12. A. Dinner. B. A snack. C. Nothing. D. Oranges.
13. A. The woman is sending a gift for Ann and the kids.
    B. Ann shares a house with the woman and her children.
    C. The conversation takes place late at night.
    D. The man doesn't want to drive in the dark.
14. A. An account. B. Cash. C. To write a check. D. To count it.
15. A. Buy a new car. B. Stay home and save their money.
    C. Fly to Las Vegas. D. Drive through the Death Valley.

Part Two Dialogue

Scientific Breakthroughs in the 21st Century

Words and Expressions

breakthrough	/'breikθruː/	*n.*	突破
evolution	/ˌiːvə'luːʃ(ə)n, ˌevə-/	*n.*	进化
genetic	/dʒi'netik/	*adj.*	基因的；遗传的
therapeutic	/ˌθerə'pjuːtik/	*adj.*	治疗的
crack	/kræk/	*v.*	揭开
virus	/'vaiərəs/	*n.*	病毒

aging	/'eidʒiŋ/	n.	衰老
reverse	/ri'vəːs/	v.	反转
DNA[缩] (deoxyribonucleic acid)		n.	[生]脱氧核糖核酸
life expectancy		n.	估计寿命

1. Listen to the dialogue and choose the best answer to each of the following questions.

1) What are they talking about in the dialogue?
   A. The history of the technology development.
   B. Scientific breakthroughs in the 21st century.
   C. Science fiction.
   D. The contribution of technology.
2) What is NOT mentioned in the dialogue?
   A. Genes. B. Universe.
   C. Environment. D. Aging.
3) How can cancer be conquered?
   A. Repair the infected cells.
   B. Repair the damaged DNA.
   C. Remove the cells infected by viruses.
   D. Replace the damaged DNA with healthy genes.
4) How can we live longer?
   A. Stop the process of aging. B. Reverse the process of aging.
   C. Control the process of aging. D. Both B and C.

2. Listen to the dialogue again and fill in the blanks with the information you hear.

1) Everything is developing at ______________.
2) It is predicted that there will be some ______________ in this century.
3) Scientists will ______________ presenting detailed picture of the ______________ from the time it was a fraction of a second old to the present.
4) That will definitely lead to longer ______________ of human beings.

3. Questions for discussion.

1) What else do you think the new century will bring us in science and technology?
2) Do you think you are lucky to live in this new century with great scientific development?

Part Three Compound Dictation

The Japanese Economy

Listen to the passage and fill in the blanks wih the information you hear.

Japan's economic expansion is showing solid strength and staying power. We are 1)____________________ that the annual growth rate of real GNP for both this year and the next will be in the four-to-five-percent range. In particular, for this year as a whole, it will wind up at the high end of that 2)____________________.

In the first quarter, real GNP growth dropped off 3)____________________ to an annual rate of only four-tenths of one percent. But that is no cause for alarm; Japan's growth rate swings very widely from one quarter to the next, and there are already many 4)____________________ that it has swung back up in the second quarter.

In the fourth quarter of last year, real growth shot up at an annual 9.6%. So the 5)____________________ for the new quarters, fourth quarter and first, is 5%. But in any case, in the second quarter, which just ended, industrial output leaped back up at an 6)____________________ rate of 11.8% — after a first-quarter decline of 2.7%. So you see, the 7)____________________ remains strong and you can expect it to stay on track.

8)____. That was to be expected. But even at this slower pace, export growth will remain a pillar of the economic expansion.

But now the expansion is also drawing strength from a recovery in domestic demand and from a continuing vigor in capital spending. 9)____
____.
With inflation running below 2%, the result has been a gradual recovery in consumer sales and in spending on travel and entertaining.

But perhaps a more positive factor has been resilient (有弹性的) strength in capital spending. Its tempo (发展速度) has slowed a bit. The semiconductor (半导体) industry, for instance, has trimmed its capital spending plans because demand for its products has slowed. 10)____. Still, across the economy, corporate profits are way up , and we expect that this year, in real terms, capital spending will rise 7% – 8%.

Part Four Passages

A. E-money

Words and Expressions

e-money		n.	电子钞票
slot	/slɔt/	n.	槽

deduct	/di'dʌkt/	*vt.*	扣除
debit	/'debit/	*n.*	借款
reckoning	/'rekəniŋ/	*n.*	算账
bill	/bil/	*v.*	通告
transaction	/træn'zækʃ(ə)n, trɑː-/	*n.*	交易
verify	/'verifai/	*v.*	查证，核实
problematic	/ˌprɔblə'mætik/	*adj.*	成问题的
frustration	/frʌ'streiʃ(ə)n/	*n.*	受挫
versatile	/'vəːsətail/	*adj.*	万能的，通用的
smart card			智能卡
vending machine			自动售货机

1. Listen to the passage and choose the best answer to complete the following sentences.

1) E-money refers to ____________.
   A. credit cards　　B. greenbacks
   C. smart cards　　D. checks

2) With a smart card, you will be able to ____________.
   A. board a bus
   B. buy a cool drink from a vending machine
   C. pay for breakfast at a restaurant
   D. all of the above

3) All the following statements are true except that ____________.
   A. a smart card is convenient and secure

B. a smart card is more convenient than a credit card

C. the value of a smart card must be verified by phone

D. when the value of a smart card is reduced or exhausted, you can add money on it

4) The passage mainly tells us __________.

A. both the advantages and disadvantages of smart cards

B. the problems of vending machines

C. the disadvantages of credit cards and checks

D. the advantages of smart cards

2. Listen to the passage again and decide whether the following statements are true (T) or false (F).

(   ) 1) You can add value to a smart card by inserting it in the vending machine.

(   ) 2) E-money will be accepted as universally as dollars very soon.

(   ) 3) Even modern vending machines will reject bills because of folded corners and wrinkled edges.

(   ) 4) The value of a smart card can be verified and changed without going through the kind of credit card dial-up system.

(   ) 5) The society in the future will turn out to be a cashless one.

B. The US Economy

Words and Expressions

rebound	/ri'baund/	*n.*	反弹
malaise	/mæ'leiz/	*n.*	隐忧；不安
damp	/dæmp/	*vt.*	抑制；降低
sluggish	/'slʌgiʃ/	*adj.*	缓慢的
recession	/ri'seʃ(ə)n/	*n.*	衰退

overextend	/'əuvəiks'tend/	*v.*	使冒过大的风险；放账过多
creditworthy	/'kreditwəːði/	*adj.*	有资格接受信贷的
contention	/kən'tenʃ(ə)n/	*n.*	争议；争论
perceive	/pə'siːv/	*v.*	察觉；领悟
grind	/graind/	*v.*	磨光；磨碎
halt	/hɔːlt/	*n.*	停止
enhancing	/in'hɑːnsiŋ/	*n.*	增强
boost	/buːst/	*v.*	促进
pessimist	/'pesimist/	*n.*	悲观者
head to			导致
zig and zag			急转；突变
real capital outlay			实际资本支出
break-even point			盈亏平衡点

1. Listen to the passage and choose the best answer to complete each of the following sentences.

1) Generally, economists have fallen into two camps in viewing ____________.

A. the economic performance

B. the strength of the service sector

C. the strength of the auto industry

D. the strength of the construction industry

2) Some economists are pessimistic when they feel that ____________.

A. the market demand would be too large

B. the real GNP would decline significantly

C. there could be a recession

D. investment in capital goods would rise too fast

3) According to the speaker, the continuing rise in consumer real income may lead to ________.

A. an increase in lending | B. an increase in borrowing
C. a reduction in lending | D. a reduction in borrowing

4) In your judgement, the speaker is ________ about the economic outlook.

A. pessimistic | B. optimistic
C. conservative | D. sceptical

2. Listen to the passage and decide whether the following sentences are true (T) or false (F).

( ) 1) Debt always rises faster than income during economic recession years.

( ) 2) Over the last 20 years, both consumer credit and consumer income have generally risen at a similar pace.

( ) 3) Some analysts perceive that the weakness in the economy and in corporate profits will discourage people from investing.

( ) 4) Now the investment tends to building new capacity.

3. Talk with your partner(s) and comment on American gross domestic product (GDP) according to the following chart.

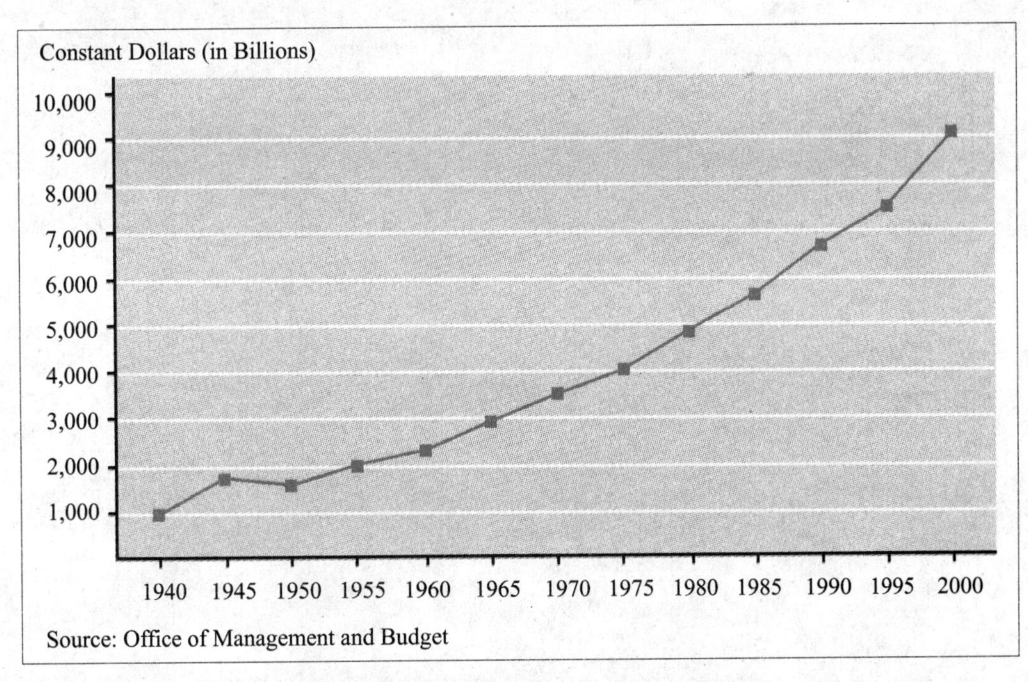

Gross Domestic Product (GDP), the United States

Unit Ten Chinese Culture

Part One Short Conversations

Listen to the following short conversations and choose the best answer to each question you hear.

1. A. Rest for a few hours. B. Go to the concert.
   C. Send a telegram. D. Go to get some tickets for the concert.
2. A. At the airport. B. At the hotel.
   C. At the railway station. D. At the cinema.
3. A. Tom's parents will leave for Los Angeles on Monday.
   B. Tom has left for Los Angeles.
   C. Tom has decided not to go to Los Angeles.
   D. Tom's parents went to Los Angeles.
4. A. \$6.80. B. \$7.20. C. \$3.15. D. \$6.30.
5. A. It ran into another car. B. It fell into a river.
   C. It was badly damaged. D. It left the road and landed in a field.
6. A. She learned to drive at 16. B. She never takes buses.
   C. She can drive a car now. D. She always takes buses.
7. A. At 4:15. B. At 4:00. C. At 4:45. D. At 5:00.

8. A. She'll go to the dance party. B. She'll type a paper.
C. She'll go to a history class. D. She'll type a letter.

9. A. $12. B.$14. C.$24. D.$30.

10. A. He is working in a hospital.
B. He is doing business with his brother now.
C. He is going to graduate from college in July.
D. He is going to do business with his brother.

11. A. A writer. B. A publisher. C. A teacher. D. A student.

12. A. Not apologetic. B. Not responsible.
C. Bewildered. D. Broken-hearted.

13. A. Read the woman's magazine. B. Subscribe to the magazine right away.
C. Buy the first issue of a magazine. D. Start a new magazine.

14. A. She should take it to the post office. B. It is too big to send by mail.
C. She should return it to the sender. D. It needs more stamps.

15. A. It's raining. B. She doesn't want to get sunburned.
C. It's not a sunny day. D. It's not warm enough outside.

Part Two Dialogue

China Culture Week

Words and Expressions

millennium	/mi'leniəm/	*n.*	一千年
essence	/'esns/	*n.*	精华
pottery	/'pɔtəri/	*n.*	陶器
costume	/'kɔstjuːm/	*n.*	服装
relic	/'relik/	*n.*	遗迹；废墟
unearth	/'ʌn'əːθ/	*v.*	掘出
embrace	/im'breis/	*v.*	包含
exposition	/ˌekspə'ziʃ(ə)n/	*n.*	博览会，展览会
oriental	/ˌɔri'entl/	*adj.*	东方的

symbolic	/sim'bɔlik/	*adj.*	象征的
ethnic	/'eθnik/	*adj.*	种族的，民族的
accessory	/æk'sesəri/	*n.*	装饰品
martial arts			武术

1. Listen to the dialogue and choose the best answer to each of the following questions.

1) What do we know about the coming China Culture Week?

   A. It's a performance that lasts seven days.

   B. It's a cultural exchange activity.

   C. It's the first activity of its kind.

   D. It's the largest exhibition China has ever held.

2) Where will the exhibition be held?

   A. In Europe.

   B. In China.

   C. In the UK.

   D. In Beijing.

3) What's NOT the purpose of the China Culture Week?

   A. To celebrate the arrival of the new millennium.

   B. To promote the exchange between China and the UK.

   C. To enhance understanding between the East and the West.

   D. To help British people know more about China.

4) Which of the following will NOT be included in the exhibition?

   A. Chinese pottery.

   B. The achievements of China's education.

   C. The new outlook of Shanghai.

   D. Beijing Opera.

5) What do you know about Beijing Opera from the interview?

   A. It originated from Beijing in Han dynasty.

   B. Many famous models from the mainland are interested in Beijing Opera.

   C. The Chinese garment industry and Chinese designers contributed a lot to its development.

   D. It's also known as "Oriental Opera".

2. Listen to the dialogue again and answer the following questions.

1) What are the purposes of staging China Culture Week?

a) ______________________________

b) ______________________________

2) What will be displayed in the week?

____

3) What are the two major types of activities in the coming week?

a) ______________________________

b) ______________________________

4) When and where did Beijing Opera originate?

____

5) What will be included in the display of 600 sets of clothes?

a) ______________________________

b) ______________________________

c) ______________________________

3. If you were in charge of a China Culture week, what activities would you select? Write down at least three.

1) ______________________________

2) ______________________________

3) ______________________________

Part Three Compound Dictation

Traditional Celebration of the Chinese New Year

Listen to the passage and fill in the blanks with the information you hear.

Of all the traditional Chinese festivals, the Chinese New Year is perhaps the most 1) ____________, colorful, and important. This is a time for the Chinese to 2) ____________ each other and themselves on having passed through another year, a time to finish out the old, and to welcome in the New Year.

The Chinese New Year is celebrated on the first day of the First Moon of the lunar calendar. The 3) ________________ date in the solar calendar varies from as early as January 21st to as late as February 19th. Chinese New Year, as the Western New Year, signifies turning over a new leaf. Socially, it is a time for family 4) ________________, and for visiting friends and relatives. This holiday, more than any other Chinese holiday, 5) ________________ the importance of family 6) ________________. The Chinese New Year's Eve dinner gathering is among the most important family 7) ________________ of the year.

8) ____ ____. The 20th of the Twelfth Moon is set aside for the annual housecleaning, or the "sweeping of the grounds". 9) ____ ____ ________________. Spring Couplets (对联), written in black ink on large vertical scrolls of red paper, are put on the walls or on the sides of the gate-ways. These couplets, short poems written in Classical Chinese, are expressions of good wishes for the family in the coming year. 10) ____ ____ ____.

Part Four Passages

A. Lu Xun

Words and Expressions

foremost	/'fɔːməust/	*adj.*	最重要的
exert	/ig'zəːt/	*v.*	尽力；发挥
abruptly	/ə'brʌptli/	*adv.*	突然
endeavor	/in'devə/	*n.*	努力
renown	/ri'naun/	*n.*	名声
initiate	/i'niʃieit/	*v.*	开始；发动
contemporary	/kən'tempərəri/	*adj.*	当代的
vernacular	/və'nækjulə/	*n.*	日常用语；白话
devastating	/'devəsteitiŋ/	*adj.*	讽刺的
critique	/kri'tiːk/	*n.*	批评
hail	/heil/	*v.*	向……欢呼；致敬
torment	/'tɔːment/	*v.*	痛苦；折磨
inner	/'inə/	*adj.*	内心的

pessimism	/'pesimizm/	*n.*	悲观
stance	/stæns/	*n.*	姿态
genre	/'ʒɑːnrə/	*n.*	类型；流派
cosmopolitan	/ˌkɔzmə'pɔlitən/	*adj.*	世界性的
reminiscence	/ˌremi'nisns/	*n.*	回忆
mental depression			精神抑郁

1. Please tick the statements that are true according to what you have heard about Lu Xun.

( ) 1) Lu Xun was born in a city in Northern China.

( ) 2) In 1916 he went to Japan to study medicine.

( ) 3) Lu Xun is generally acknowledged as a leader of the May Fourth Movement.

( ) 4) Lu Xun was a pioneer of Communist thought.

( ) 5) Lu Xun wrote Diary of a Madman in 1919.

( ) 6) He founded the League of Left-Wing Writers.

( ) 7) In addition to his short stories, Lu Xun also produced 60 volumes of essays.

( ) 8) Lu Xun also produced about 50 poems in the classical style.

( ) 9) He had once taught Chinese literature at universities in Beijing.

( ) 10) Throughout his creative life, Lu Xun was deeply tormented by a conflict between his inner pessimism and his public stance in favor of building a new Chinese nation and society.

2. Listen to the passage again and complete the following chart.

Time	Major Events in Lu Xun's Life
1902	
1906	
1909	
1918	
in the 1920s	
toward the end of his life	

Words and Expressions

formula	/'fɔːmjulə/	*n.*	公式；客套语
incomprehensible	/ˌinkɔmpri'hensəbl/	*adj.*	不能理解的
frustrate	/frʌs'treit/	*vt.*	挫败；使感到灰心
gender	/'dʒendə/	*n.*	[语] 性
case	/keis/	*n.*	[语] 格
number	/'nʌmbə/	*n.*	[语] 数
tense	/tens/	*n.*	[语] 时态
voice	/vɔis/	*n.*	[语] 语态
mood	/muːd/	*n.*	[语] 语气
agreement	/ə'griːmənt/	*n.*	[语] (人称、数、格等的)一致
pride oneself on			为……而得意

1. Listen to the passage and choose the best answer to each of the following questions.

1) What did he sound like when the person who is very "good at" learning Chinese introduced his wife in Chinese?

A. This is my piece of cheese. B. This is my piece of chips.

C. This is my piece of chess. D. This is my piece of chick.

2) In which aspect will the friend of the speaker find the Chinese language differs most from the English language?

A. The word order. B. Grammar.

C. The spelling. D. The tone of the words.

3) What feature do the Chinese language and the English language have in common?

A. They both depend very much on word order.

B. They both depend very much on tenses.

C. They both depend very much on spelling.

D. They both depend very much on way of writing.

4) What do we know about the grammar of the Chinese language from the passage?

A. There are various answers representing two contradictory views.

B. There are various answers representing two complementary views.

C. There are various answers representing three contradictory views.

D. There are various answers representing three contradictory views.

5) What do foreigners tend to think about the Chinese language?

A. There seems to be many rules about the Chinese language.

B. There seems to be no rules about the Chinese language.

C. There seems to be only one rule about the Chinese language.

D. There seems to be three rules about the Chinese language.

2. Listen to the passage again and fill in the blanks with the information you hear.

I have a friend who rather prides himself on his talent for learning foreign languages. He said that when he first came to China he learned to 1) ______________ of all the impossible Chinese sounds within a matter of weeks.

Now this friend of mine is not 2) ______________, so he decided he would 3) ______________. But when the time came for him to try that out, he found to his disappointment again that people thought 4) ______________.

These answers represent 5) ______________. One view is that Chinese is a language without grammar. Because the Chinese nouns and pronouns have 6) ______________ and the Chinese verbs have 7) ______________. There is 8) ______________________________, no strict pattern of a grammatical sentence, and not even 9) ______________________________. In fact, there is no anything. They make Chinese sound like 10) ______________________________.

3. Questions for discussion.

1) Which language do you think is more difficult, English or Chinese?

2) What suggestions would you like to give to foreigners who are going to study Chinese?

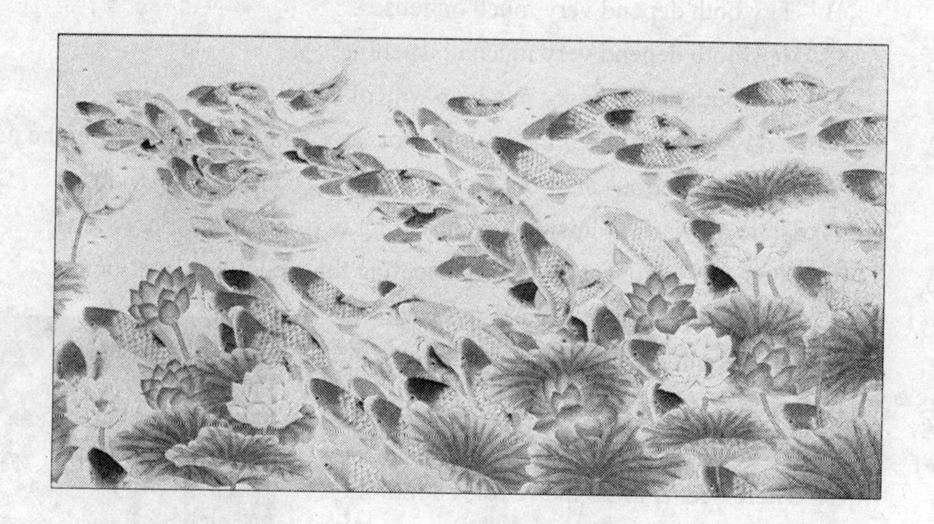

Unit Eleven Philosophy of Life

Part One Short Conversations

Listen to the following short conversations and choose the best answer to each question you hear.

1. A. He did some literature assignments. B. He returned some books.
   C. He did some shopping. D. He went to see a film.
2. A. Write letters to her. B. Take care of her house.
   C. Collect her letters. D. Look after her pet.
3. A. She has to watch her weight. B. She doesn't like sweet things.
   C. She is too full to eat anything else. D. She would like something else.
4. A. They should wait longer for Jane. B. Jane probably won't come.
   C. He forgot to tell Jane to come. D. Jane is very busy.
5. A. Liz is on a business tour. B. Ted takes Liz for a holiday.
   C. Ted is gone for a holiday. D. Ted usually gives a ride to Liz.
6. A. She works part-time this term.
   B. She wants to become a scholar.
   C. She needn't work part-time this term.
   D. Her grades ware not good enough for a scholarship.

7. A. By car. B. By train. C. By bus. D. By taxi.
8. A. It's 5 minutes fast. B. It's 5 minutes slow.
   C. It's 40 minutes fast. D. It doesn't work.
9. A. He went to class late.
   B. He was not interested in the course.
   C. He had to go to other courses at the same time.
   D. It was too late for him to sign up for the course.
10. A. A professor. B. A doctor. C. A dentist. D. A manager.
11. A. The house is expensive. B. The man wants to sell it.
    C. This house is worthy buying. D. The lady wants to buy it.
12. A. Sex. B. Age. C. Quality. D. Appearance.
13. A. The man wants to cut down his weight.
    B. The man doesn't want to eat more because he is full.
    C. The man has no appetite.
    D. The man is very shy to eat more because he is very fat.
14. A. She is taking a picture of the man.
    B. She is ordering the man to take some cheese.
    C. She is asking the man to wait for her cheese.
    D. She is showing the man how to make cheese.
15. A. Not bad. B. Terrible. C. Excellent. D. Just so-so.

Part Two
Dialogue

Most Important Thing Is to Be Happy

Words and Expressions

settle down	安顿下来
start a family	建立家庭
put roots into the ground	(到一个新地方)落地生根，扎根

1. Listen to the dialogue and give a tick (√) to sentences which are correct about Mrs. Lee's son according to what you have heard.

(　) 1) He is over 30 years old.

(　) 2) He is quite different from other young people.

(　) 3) He is dating a girl he loves and wants to marry her.

(　) 4) He intends to find a new job and earn more money.

(　) 5) He seldom talks with his mother.

(　) 6) No one knows what he's thinking about.

2. Listen to the dialogue again and complete the following chart.

	Mrs. Lee's View	Carl's View
Job and Money		
Love and Family		

3. Questions for discussion.

1) What do you think of the life of Linda's son?

2) What kind of love do you think is natural love?

Part Three Compound Dictation

Bias for Beauty

Listen to the passage and fill in the blanks with the information you hear.

We are all more obsessed with our appearance than we like to admit. But this is not an 1) ________________ of "vanity". Vanity means conceit, excessive pride in one's appearance. Concern about appearance is quite normal and 2) ________________.
Attractive people have 3) ________________ advantages in our society. Attractive children are more popular, both with classmates and teachers. Attractive 4) ________________ have a better chance of getting jobs, and of receiving higher salaries.

We also believe in the "what is beautiful is good" stereotype — an 5) ________________ but deep-seated belief that physically attractive people possess other desirable characteristics such as intelligence, 6) ________________, social skills, confidence — even moral 7) ________________. The good fairy is always beautiful; the wicked stepmother is always ugly.

8) ____
________________________________.

Concern with appearance is not just a phenomenon of Modern Western Culture. Every period of history has had its own standards of what is and is not beautiful, and every contemporary society has its own distinctive concept of the ideal physical attributes. Now we try to diet and exercise ourselves into the fashionable shape — often with even more serious consequences. 9) ____

____.

Advances in technology and in particular the rise of the mass media has caused normal concerns about how we look to become obsessions.

Even very attractive people may not be looking in the mirror out of "vanity", but out of insecurity. We forget that there are disadvantages to being attractive: attractive people are under much greater pressure to maintain their appearance. Also, studies show that attractive people don't benefit from the "bias for beauty" in terms of self-esteem. 10) ____________________

____

____

____

____

____________________.

Part Four Passages

A. Laziness

Words and Expressions

immoral	/i'mɔrəl/	*adj.*	不道德的
distrustful	/dis'trʌstful/	*adj.*	不信任的
ridicule	/'ridikjuːl/	*n.*	嘲笑，奚落
orchard	/'ɔːtʃəd/	*n.*	果园
tempt	/tempt/	*v.*	试探；吸引
contemplate	/'kɔntempleit/	*v.*	沉思
goof off			游手好闲；不认真工作
take time off			抽出一部分时间

1. Listen to the passage and choose the best answer to each of the following questions.

1) What's the main idea of the passage?

   A. Laziness is a moral sin.

   B. There are advantages and disadvantages in being lazy.

   C. Laziness is the sign of deep-seated emotional problems.

   D. Lazy people do more careful work.

2) Which of the following statements can be inferred from the passage?

   A. Laziness is a disease.

   B. Laziness is more beneficial than harmful.

   C. Some people appear lazy because they are insecure.

   D. A good definition of laziness is emotional illness.

3) Why is laziness helpful?

   A. Because all great scientific discoveries occurred by chance or while someone was "goofing off".

   B. Because most great scientific discoveries occurred by chance or while someone was "goofing off".

   C. Because lazy people are always avoiding hard work.

   D. Taking time off for a rest is good for the overworked student.

4) Which of the following words can best describe the speaker's tone at the end of the passage?

   A. philosophical　　　　B. humorous

C. serious D. commonsense

5) Which of the following conclusion does the passage support?

A. The word laziness is sometimes applied incorrectly.

B. Most of the time laziness is a virtue.

C. People should be lazy.

D. Most insecure people are lazy.

2. Listen to the passage again and answer the following questions.

1) What do people generally think of laziness?

____

2) What are much more serious problems for some people who appear to be lazy?

____

3) What does Newton's example show?

____

4) For whom is taking a rest useful?

____

3. What's your attitude toward laziness now?

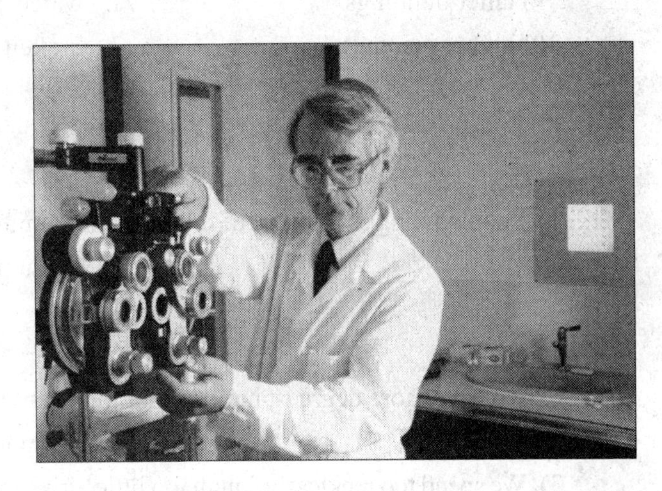

B. Paradox of Our Times

Words and Expressions

paradox	/'pærədɔks/	*n.*	似非而是的论点；自相矛盾的话
inconceivable	/ˌinkən'siːvəbl/	*adj.*	难以相信的

steep	/stiːp/	*adj.*	不合理的
wellness	/'welnis/	*n.*	健康
recklessly	/'reklisli/	*adv.*	鲁莽地；不顾一切地
freeway	/'friːwei/	*n.*	高速公路
short temper			急性子；脾气暴躁

1. Listen to the passage and match Column A with Column B to make a paradox according to what you have heard.

Column A	Column B
1) fast foods	A. less nutrition
2) steep profits	B. shallow relationships
3) more kinds of food	C. more divorce
4) more conveniences	D. slow digestion
5) two incomes	E. less wellness
6) fancier houses	F. shorter tempers
7) more medicine	G. less time
8) read too little	H. lower morals
9) taller buildings	I. watch TV too often
10) higher incomes	J. broken homes

2. Listen to the passage again and fill in the blanks with the information you hear.

1) People living at the start of the third millennium enjoy a world that would have been ______________________. Human beings are faced with ______________________.

2) We have ______________________; more conveniences, but less time; we have more degrees, but less common sense; more knowledge, but less judgment; ______________________; more medicine, but less wellness.

3) We spend too recklessly, laugh too little, drive too fast, ______________________, stay up too late, get up too tired, read too little, watch TV too often, and ______________________.

4) We have ______________________, but reduced our values. We talk too much, love too little and lie too often. We've learned how to make a living, but not a life; we've ______________________, not life to years.

5) We've been all the way to the moon and back, but have trouble ______________________. We've conquered outer space, but ______________________. We've split the atom, but ______________________; we write more,

but learn less; plan more, but ________________.

6) We build more computers to ________________, to produce more copies, but have less communication. We are long on quantity, but ________________.

3. Translate the following paradoxes into Chinese.

1) These are the times of fast foods and slow digestion; tall men and short character; steep profits and shallow relationships.
2) We have more degrees, but less common sense; more knowledge, but less judgment; more experts, but more problems; more medicine, but less wellness.
3) We've learned how to make a living, but not a life; we've added years to life, not life to years.
4) We've been all the way to the moon and back, but have trouble crossing the street to meet the new neighbor.
5) We build more computers to hold more information, to produce more copies, but have less communication.

Unit Twelve Law

Part One Short Conversations

Listen to the following short conversations and choose the best answer to each question you hear.

1. A. In a library. B. In a hospital.
   C. In a restaurant. D. In a drugstore.
2. A. She is not a pleasant person. B. She does not talk very much.
   C. She is very nice. D. She is pleasant to talk with.
3. A. She didn't stay in her cabin.
   B. She suffered from sea sickness during the trip.
   C. She enjoyed her trip on the ocean liner.
   D. She ate too much during the trip.
4. A. A television set. B. A washing machine.
   C. A public telephone. D. A candy machine.
5. A. In New York City. B. In his sister's home.
   C. In Greece. D. On a plane.
6. A. To a restaurant. B. To a hotel.
   C. To a hospital. D. To a store.

7. A. Weights and measures. B. The government.
   C. The cost of living. D. Science classes.
8. A. She has bought a new one. B. She has none at present.
   C. She has only an old one. D. Her sister has given her one.
9. A. Fifteen dollars. B. Twelve dollars.
   C. Four dollars. D. Five dollars.
10. A. Candy. B. Toys.
    C. Cigarettes. D. Books.
11. A. The man will buy it. B. It's too expensive.
    C. The man is dissatisfied with it. D. The man will not buy it.
12. A. The man is very sad with his examination.
    B. The man's IQ is so low that he could not pass the examination.
    C. Somebody is worse than him.
    D. The woman is trying to encourage him.
13. A. The man and woman are policeman and stranger.
    B. The man and woman are lovers.
    C. The man and woman are father and daughter.
    D. The man and woman are husband and wife.
14. A. Where does the girl come from? B. Why do you love such a girl?
    C. How do you love her? D. How do you know the girl?
15. A. They are talking about the quality. B. The man is showing his discontent.
    C. They are discussing the price. D. The woman is paying the man.

Part Two Dialogue

Should Handguns Be Banned?

Words and Expressions

insane	/in'sein/	*adj.*	患精神病的；极愚蠢的
outlaw	/'autlɔː/	*vt.*	取缔；宣布……为非法
ban	/bæn/	*vt.*	禁止；取缔

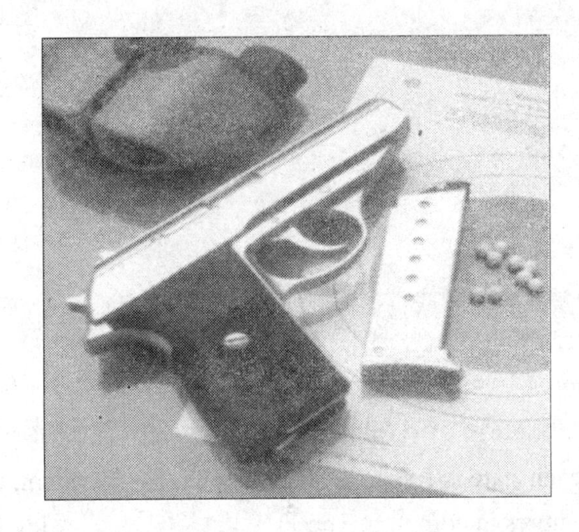

1. Listen to the dialogue and find out Mike and Helen's opinions about owning handguns. Mark your answer with a tick (✓) in the chart.

	For	Against
Mike		
Helen		

2. Listen to the dialogue again and list the reasons for their different opinions.

Mike: ______________________________

____

____

Helen: ______________________________

____

____

3. What's your opinion of owning handguns? Ask your partner whether he/she thinks citizens should be allowed to own handguns.

Part Three Compound Dictation

The Court System in the USA

Listen to the passage and fill in the blanks with the information you hear.

Although each state is free to arrange its own court system, most states justice systems have several features in common. The 1) ________ level court in trials where state law is alleged (断言，宣称) to have been 2) ________ is the trial court. This is the only court with the power to 3) ________ the actual facts involved in a case. If either party involved in the case feels that the trial 4) ________ made an error in one of his rulings, they can 5) ________, or bring the case to a Court of Appeals. Whereas trials are focused around the testimony (证据，证明) of 6) ________ concerning their actions or observations, appeals feature two attorneys 7) ________ to convince a panel (专门小组) of five judges that the law favors their side. 8) ________________________. Attorneys prepare written briefs citing historical precedents and rulings to persuade the panel of judges to rule in their favor. If unsatisfied with the court's ruling (裁决), a party can ask for a Writ of Certiorari, which is essentially an appeal to the state Supreme Court. 9) ________________________.

Out of the approximately 5,000 cases each year appealed to the United States Supreme Court, it actually hears between 100–125 of them. The procedure at this level is similar to that at the appeals court; each attorney addresses the panel of Justices, which can interrupt at almost any time with questions. 10) ________________________.

Part Four
Passages

A. What Is A Lawyer?

Words and Expressions

uphold	/ʌp'həuld/	*vt.*	坚持；维护
enact	/i'nækt/	*vt.*	颁布；通过(法案等)
accredit	/ə'kredit/	*v.*	鉴定……为合格
take an oath			宣誓
real estate			不动产；房地产
legal matters			法律事务
professional ethics			职业道德
settle disputes			解决分歧，解决争端
intellectural property			知识产权

1. Listen to the passage and decide whether the following statements are true (T) or false (F).

(　) 1) A lawyer usually spends less time in an office than in a courtroom.

(　) 2) Laws don't change constantly, and new cases regularly alter the meanings of laws.

(　) 3) A lawyer has two main duties: to uphold the law and protect a client's rights.

(　) 4) A lawyer must have both knowledge of the law and good communication skills.

(　) 5) A person is required to meet the standards enacted by the state before he or she is licensed to practice the law.

2. Listen to the passage again and list the standards that any licensed lawyer must meet.

1) ____________________

2) ____________________

3) ____________________

4) ____________________

5) ____________________

6) ____________________

Graldine Ferraro, lawyer

William Evarts, lawyer

B. The Congress

Words and Expressions

legislative	/'ledʒis,leitiv/	*adj.*	立法的
designation	/,dezig'neiʃən/	*n.*	名称，称号
consent	/kən'sent/	*n.*	同意
nomination	/,nɔmi'neiʃən/	*n.*	任命
amendment	/ə'mendmənt/	*n.*	修正案
impeachment	/im'piːtʃmənt/	*n.*	弹劾
parliamentary body			议会团体
the Senate			参议院
the House of Representatives			众议院
appropriation bill			拨款法
revenue bill			税法
the grand jury			(由12至13人组成的)大陪审团

1. Listen to the passage and choose the best answer to each of the following questions.

1) What is the chief function of the Congress?

A. Making laws.

B. Advising and consenting to treaties.

C. Deciding on presidential elections.

D. Trying the impeachment.

2) When do both houses meet in joint session, following a presidential election to count the electoral votes?

A. On the sixth day of December.

B. On the sixteenth day of January.

C. On the sixth day of January.

D. On the sixteenth day of December.

3) Who presents the charges in the matter of impeachments?

A. The Senate.

B. The House of Representatives.

C. The President.

D. The Vice-President.

4) How many votes can remove an impeached person from his post?

A. One third of the House of Representatives.

B. Two-thirds of the House of Representatives.

C. One-third of the Senate.

D. Two-thirds of the Senate.

2. Listen to the passage again and fill in the blanks with the information you hear.

Unlike some other 1) ____________________, both the Senate and the House of Representatives have 2) ____________ ____________ with certain exceptions. For example, the Constitution provides that only the House of Representatives 3) ____________________. By tradition, the House also originates 4) ____________________. As both bodies have 5) ____________ ____________, the designation of one as the "upper" House and the other

as the "lower" House is 6) ______________________.

3. Discuss with your classmate how the Congress will act if no candidate receives a majority of the total electoral votes in the presidential election.

TAPESCRIPTS AND KEYS

Unit One Education

Part One Short Conversations

1. D 2. C 3. D 4. B 5. C 6. C 7. A 8. C
9. A 10. B 11. B 12. C 13. C 14. B 15. B

Tapescript

1. *W*: How much is this box of candy?
   M: Let's see. The two-pound box is five dollars. You're holding a three-pound box, so it's two dollars more.
   Q: How much will the box of candy cost the woman?
2. *M*: The speed limit on interstate highway is 55 miles per hour.
   W: But Janet was going 20 miles per hour over that.
   Q: How fast was Janet driving?
3. *W*: Betty lost two pounds on her diet, and Jones lost three.
   M: Bill lost twice as much as the two of them.
   Q: How much weight did Bill lose?
4. *W*: I was in the gas station at 1:00. How did I miss you?
   M: I got there at a quarter to 12:00 and waited a while. But I guess I left before you got there.
   Q: When did the man probably leave the gas station?
5. *W*: Every time I see you, Bob, you are wearing a different tie.
   M: That's because I have one for everyday of the week.
   Q: How many ties does the man have?
6. *M*: My library book is ten days overdue. Can you tell me how much I owe you?
   W: Let's see. Ten days at 5 cents a day will cost you 50 cents.
   Q: How much does the man owe the woman?
7. *M*: How much does it cost to bowl here?
   W: It's usually 75 cents a game, but today there's a special 60-cent a game.
   Q: How much will it cost to bowl 5 games today?
8. *M*: I'd like to buy these four Thanksgiving cards. Are they 10 cents each?

W: Three of them are, but that smaller one is only a nickel.

Q: How much are the cards together?

9. W: Why are you giving me a ticket for speeding, officer? I was only going 40.

M: Can't you read? That was 10 miles per hour over the limit.

Q: What is the speed limit in this area?

10. M: When I'm 65, I will start getting Social Security payments from the government.

W: That means the first checks will start to arrive about three years from now and you can quit your job.

Q: How old is the man now?

11. W: I'm sure glad I don't have your job, working all night and sleeping in the daytime.

M: Oh, I stopped that when I got my promotion. Now I'm on three days and off two.

Q: How does the man work now?

12. W: Excuse me. When will the 7:15 bus arrive?

M: It's been delayed two hours because a bridge was broken.

Q: What do we learn from this conversation?

13. M: How many people will be coming to the reunion on Saturday?

W: We had to cross off fifteen names from our original list of one hundred.

Q: How many people do they expect to attend the reunion?

14. W: How long did you have for the exam?

M: We were allotted two hours, but I finished in less than half the time.

Q: How much time did the student take for the exam?

15. M: I'd like to pick this film up at 4 tomorrow afternoon.

W: I can have it for you at 2, if you like.

Q: What does the woman say about the film?

Part Two Dialogue

Education in Canada

1. 1) T 2) T 3) F 4) F 5) T 6) F 7) T 8) T

2. 1) elementary and secondary schooling

2) 13 years

3) at the end of grade11

4) undertake university studies

5) general and vocational education

Tapescript

A: I'm interested in how children are educated in Canada.

B: Education is compulsory from ages 5 to 16.

A: Is it free?

B: Yes, up to the end of secondary school, that is about age 18.

A: What do you mean by "secondary" school?

B: Early school, that is, primary grade to about grade 8, is called "elementary" school. Above that, up to grade 12, is called "secondary" school. Post-secondary education, university and professional training, are sometimes called "tertiary" education.

A: In China we have two streams in high school, sciences and liberal arts.

B: Canada also has two streams in high school, academic and commercial. But university entrance may be gained only from the academic stream.

A: I heard that some parents pay for their children's education in Canada.

B: Yes. If you're not satisfied with the public school system, you can send your children to private school which may possibly give a better education.

A: Is it expensive?

B: Yes, sometimes more expensive than university, especially if it's a boarding school.

A: Do children educated privately have an equal chance at university entrance?

B: Yes, equal if not better.

A: Do they have to pass a university entrance exam?

B: Generally not, but they must achieve a minimum level in their final exams at secondary school to become eligible. Then the best ones are accepted, depending on the number of applicants.

A: Can those who are ineligible pay to go to a private university?

B: No, there is no such thing in Canada.

A: When do students in Canada begin their post-secondary education?

B: In general, they begin their post-secondary education at the age of 17 or 18, after 11 or 12 years of elementary and secondary schooling. But in Ontario, 13 years of study is required. In Quebec, though students complete secondary schooling at the end of grade 11, those who wish to undertake university studies must first take a 2-year pre-university program at a college of general and vocational education.

Part Three Compound Dictation

Guides to American Universities

1) accepted
2) choosing
3) apply
4) better
5) information
6) reference
7) catalogue
8) You can study the general guide at almost any American library
9) Although the general guidebook has helpful information, some of the facts may be out of date
10) The catalogue not only has more accurate current facts than the guidebook, but it also has more detailed information.

Tapescript

Do you intend to study at an American university? It takes a long time to get accepted at most American schools, perhaps as much as a year. That's why you should start choosing a school as soon as possible. It's also a good idea to apply to several different institutions, so that you'll have a better chance of acceptance at one.

There are two good ways to get the information you need. One is a general reference book called *Guide to American Colleges and Universities*. The other is the catalogue published by each school. You can study the general guide at almost any American library. This book has many useful statistics, such as the number of students, the average test scores for people accepted to the school, the number of books in the library and the number of faculty members.

Although the general guidebook has helpful information, some of the facts may be out of date. For instance, many schools raise their tuition every year. Also, schools sometimes change their requirements for entrance. To be sure that you are getting current information, write to the university and ask for its catalogue. The catalogue not only has more accurate current facts than the guidebook, but it also has more detailed information. For instance, the catalogue can tell you if there is a special foreign student adviser, what kind of housing is available.

Part Four
Passages

A. College Education in Britain

1. 1) F   2) T   3) T   4) F
2. 1) from age 5 to 16
   2) three years
   3) an additional year
   4) five years
   5) give you the right to attend a university; examines your marks and decides whether to offer you a place

Tapescript

Education is compulsory in Britain from five to sixteen years of age. After this time, students can study for their "A" level examinations and then go on to some form of further education. Entry to university is competitive and simply obtaining a pass in your "A" level examinations does not automatically give you the right to attend a university. The university first interviews you and if you are successful in the interview, it examines your marks and on the basis of these decides whether to offer you a place.

Most university courses last three years. Students studying modern languages usually spend an additional year in the country of the language they are studying. Students studying medicine do a five-year course. Some universities have examinations at the end of the first year which students have to pass to continue with their university education. They then sit their degree examination at the end of the course. Other universities have a system of continuous assessment. This means that the students' marks during the whole course count towards a degree.

The majority of students in Britain attend a university which is away from their home town. They usually live on the university campus for their first year and then move into flats or houses which they share with other students for the following years. Local education authorities award grants to cover their fees and accommodation but how much they receive depends on their parents' income.

B. Problems with US Education

1. 1) A 2) B 3) D 4) A 5) C
2. 1) various kinds of intelligence 2) standardized tests
   3) certain kind of education 4) personally and professionally
   5) the opportunities they could have had 6) in a little less constrained atmosphere
   7) what you are going to be doing 8) your own special interests

Tapescript

When I was in college I had an English major and for a while I considered going into teaching. I went through the whole student teaching process. And I eventually decided that I didn't want to do that. And I went in another direction instead. But while I was exploring the possibility of becoming a teacher, I did a lot of thinking about the way that the educational system in the Unite States is run. And I disagree with a lot of the ways that things seem to happen and have happened for a long time in our educational system. I can remember when I was in junior high and senior high school, and even as early as elementary school, the way that students would tend to get boxed in very early on in their education. Um ... and it becomes really impossible to break out of ... the classes that you are more or less tracked into when you're very young. And a lot of the decisions ... are made for you really.

Uh ... people don't seem to recognize various kinds of intelligence, they seem to just want to give standardized tests and peg you down to certain kind of education. And I think there are a lot of people, who are very intelligent, that I've known personally and professionally, have not had a lot of the opportunities they could have had if the school system was more conducive to students ... learning ... in a little less constrained atmosphere. I've always felt that a lot of classes that you're forced to take in high school are not really geared towards what you are going to be doing. There's very little emphasis on your own special interests. Uh ... everybody's sort of treated like they're the same person. Everything is very generalized. There's a lot of ... uh ... there's a lot of pressure on students to be as well rounded as possible, when I think being well rounded isn't really possible because it becomes impossible to develop any one part of yourself to any great degree. And as a result people can't get into good colleges if they you know, haven't you know scored the ... the right thing on the math section of S-A-T, even if they are brilliant and writers, and vice versa. You know, um ... people just really are not given a chance, I think, in a lot of cases.

Unit Two Human Qualities

Part One Short Conversations

1. A 2. B 3. D 4. C 5. A 6. D 7. A 8. C
9. C 10. D 11. A 12. C 13. D 14. C 15. B

Tapescript

1. *W*: Could you please tell me if Flight 858 from San Francisco will be on time?
   M: Yes, Madam. It should be arriving in about 10 minutes.
   Q: Who do you think the woman is talking to?
2. *M*: Sorry to trouble you. But is there any possibility of borrowing a blanket. I feel cold.
   W: I think we've got one. Could you wait until after take-off please?
   Q: What is the probable relationship between the two speakers?
3. *W*: How long will it take you to fix my watch?
   M: I'll call you when it's ready. But it shouldn't take longer than a week.
   Q: What is the probable relationship between the speakers?
4. *W*: Good evening, Professor David. My name is Susan Gray. I'm with the local newspaper. Do you mind if I ask you a few questions?
   M: Not at all. Go ahead, please.
   Q: What is Susan Gray?
5. *W*: Dear, I feel hungry now. How about you?
   M: So do I. Let me call room service. Hello, room service. Please send a menu to 320 right away.
   Q: Where are the two speakers?
6. *M*: I've just brought your ladder back. Thanks for lending it to me. Where shall I leave it?
   W: Just lean it against the wall there. Use the ladder again anytime.
   Q: What's the probable relationship between these two speakers?
7. *M*: Are there any more questions on this lecture? Yes, Mary?

W: Dr. Baker, do you think an independent candidate could become president?

Q: What most probably is Mary?

8. *M*: Can you stay for dinner?

   W: I'd love to. But I have to go and send some registered mail before picking up the children from school.

   Q: Where will the woman go first?

9. *M*: How about the food I ordered? I've been waiting for 20 minutes already.

   W: I'm very sorry, Sir. I will be back with your order in a minute.

   Q: What's the woman's job?

10. *W*: Excuse me, Sir. I'm going to send this parcel to London. What's the postage for it?

    M: Let me see. It's one pound and fifty.

    Q: Who is the woman most probably speaking to?

11. *W*: I often mistake Jim for Bob. Can you tell them apart?

    M: No, they look so much alike that they even confused their mother sometimes when they were young.

    Q: What is the most probable relationship between Jim and Bob?

12. *M*: Have you a table for four?

    W: Certainly, Sir. A corner table or would you rather be near the window?

    Q: What is the man doing?

13. *W*: Look at that big field of cotton. And there's a farm with some beautiful houses.

    M: You really get to know the country when you go by train, don't you?

    Q: Where did the conversation most probably take place?

14. *W*: I've been wondering what sort of clothes my husband and I are going to need for our visit. What's the weather usually like in your country in September?

    M: It's not very pleasant. I'm sorry to say, generally, there are more rainy days in September than in any other month.

    Q: What is the relationship between the two speakers?

15. *W*: How long can I keep these out?

    M: Two weeks. After that you will be fined for every day they are overdue.

    W: I guess I'd read fast.

    Q: Where does the conversation most probably take place?

Part Two
Dialogue

I Think You're in the Wrong Place

1. 1) D 2) C 3) A 4) C
2. 1) over there 2) stand where I wish
   3) barge in front of a lot of other people 4) over an hour
   5) even five minutes ago 6) brawling in public
   7) saw you push in 8) Real lawyer type
   9) feathers out of your hat 10) mean what I say

Tapescript

Lady A: Excuse me, but I think you're in the wrong place.

Lady B: Are you speaking to me?

Lady A: Yes. The end of the queue's over there. I think you've made a mistake.

Lady B: A mistake? I have the right to stand where I wish.

Lady A: Maybe. But you have no right to barge in front of a lot of other people in a queue.

Lady B: Barge, did you say?

Lady A: Yes. We've all been waiting here for over an hour.

Lady B: Well, so have I.

Lady A: Look. I don't like to contradict you but you weren't here even five minutes ago.

Lady B: I have no intention of brawling in public. Here I am and I intend to stay.

Lady A: Oh, no, oh no you can't stay. Other people here saw you push in too. Now get back to the end of the queue.

Lady B: I have every right to stay wherever I like. It's a free country, isn't it?

Lady A: Clever, very clever. Real lawyer type. Well, let me tell you, you get out of this queue and move to your proper place at the back, or I'll tear the feathers out of your hat!

Lady B: Are you threatening me?

Lady A: That's right. And I always mean what I say.

Part Three Compound Dictation

Self-reliance

1) achieving
2) usually
3) stand
4) belief
5) basic
6) aspects
7) profoundly
8) If they rely too much on the support of their families or the government or any organizations they may not be free to do what they want
9) Even if they are not truly self-reliant, most Americans believe they must at least appear to be so
10) Many people believe that such individuals are setting a bad example which may weaken the American character as a whole

Tapescript

Americans believe that individuals must learn to rely on themselves or risk losing freedom. This means achieving both financial and emotional independence from their parents as early as possible, usually by age 18 to 21. It means that Americans believe they should take care of themselves, solve their own problems, and stand on their own feet.

The strong belief in self-reliance continues today as a basic American value. This is perhaps one of the most difficult aspects of the American character to understand, but it is profoundly important. Americans believe that they must be self-reliant in order to keep their freedom. If they rely too much on the support of their families or the government or any organizations they may not be free to do what they want.

By being dependent, not only do they risk losing freedom, but also risk losing the respect of their peers (同辈人). Even if they are not truly self-reliant, most Americans believe they must at least appear to be so. In order to be in the main stream of American life — to have power and respect — an individual must be seen as self-reliant. Although receiving financial support from charity, family or the government is allowed, it is never admired. Many people believe that such individuals are setting a bad example which may weaken the American character as a whole.

Part Four Passages

A. The Four Qualities of Leadership

1. 3), 6), 8), 12)
2. 1) His vision was of a prosperous, progressive Texas.
   2) He wrote and spoke every chance he had, using powerful, compelling language.
   3) He viewed mistakes simply as an opportunity for learning.
   4) He was an honorable person, true to his word and to the people around. He always put the interests of Texas above his own.

Tapescript

Stephen Fuller Austin, the Father of Texas had four qualities that enabled him to turn a bunch of rugged individualists on the frontier into a cohesive community. These qualities are timeless, and if you embrace them, you will become better leaders.

First, have a vision. Austin certainly had a clear vision of what he wanted to achieve. In a letter written in 1829, he said, "My ambition has been to succeed in redeeming Texas from its wilderness state by ... spreading over it ... enterprise and intelligence. In doing this I hope to make the fortune of thousands and my own amongst the rest." His vision was of a prosperous, progressive Texas, and he stayed absolutely true to that goal.

Second, know how to tell others about your vision. Austin is a great example of how to communicate vision with great force and clarity. He knew how to enlist others in his great mission in the wilderness. He wrote and spoke every chance he had. By sharing his vision in powerful, compelling language, Austin helped unite rugged individualists into a colony where people from different backgrounds joined together for a greater cause.

The third leadership quality Austin had was an unshakable confidence in himself, and in the rightness of what he was doing. He never even considered the possibility of failure. He learned to recognize his strengths and compensate for his weaknesses. And he viewed mistakes simply as an opportunity for learning.

Fourth, lead by example — be men and women of character. By his own character and integrity, Austin knew how to gain the people's trust. Texas knew from the way he lived his life that he was an honorable person, true to his word and to the people around. He always put the interests of Texas above his own.

It was because of these four qualities of leadership — vision, the ability to communicate that vision, confidence, and integrity — that Stephen F. Austin accomplished so much in the seedtime of Texas history. He is justly called the Father of Texas.

B. Diana, Princess of Wales

1.

When	Where	What
1987	Britain	She shook hands with AIDS patients.
1990s	...	She was involved in the international efforts to ban landmines.
in the month of her death	Bosnia	She highlighted the suffering caused by appalling left-overs of war.

2. 1) human qualities; break down barriers; break taboos
   2) the most photographed woman; an icon of fashion; remarkable instinct
   3) mental health; learning disabilities; public consciousness
   4) instinctive communicator; all walks of life

Tapescript

When Diana, Princess of Wales, once stated that "someone's got to go out there and love people and show it", she was not just revealing one of her many human qualities. This also showed her willingness to break down barriers between people; and even to break taboos.

She was the most photographed woman in the world. Yet belying her image as an icon of fashion, she supported causes regarded by many as anything but fashionable and, with remarkable instinct, transformed perceptions of these. When opening the first specialist Aids unit at a British hospital in 1987, the princess made a point of being photographed shaking hands with patients. That she wore no gloves gave rise to a controversy that today seems unbelievable — but it seems unbelievable largely because of her actions that day. In the 1990s she became involved in the international efforts to ban landmines, a campaign which had previously received little support. She visited Bosnia in the month of her death and highlighted the suffering caused by these appalling left-overs of war. And it was her commitment to other often overlooked causes such as mental health, homelessness, drugs and learning disabilities that had a similar impact on public consciousness.

Allied to her great compassion was the gift of communication. She was an instinctive communicator who could relate to people of all ages and from all walks of life. From world leaders to street children, she simply captivated all those she met. These rare gifts, her enduring human qualities, are surely how we will remember her in the years to come.

Unit Three Management

Part One Short Conversations

1. B 2. D 3. B 4. B 5. A 6. A 7. B 8. C
9. D 10. B 11. A 12. C 13. C 14. B 15. B

Tapescript

1. *M*: Did you see Ted's mother today?
   W: Actually, I saw his mother and his father.
   Q: What does the woman imply?
2. *M*: How many students will Prof. Smith choose to go on the field trip?
   W: Whether or not there'll be a field trip has to be decided first.
   Q: What does the woman mean?
3. *W*: Harvey doesn't seem to fit into this class.
   M: No, he's really a fish out of water.
   Q: What does the man mean?
4. *M*: Cooking for yourself is a lot better than eating dormitory food.
   W: You can say that again!
   Q: What does the woman mean?
5. *M*: Help me with this stack of books, will you, Jack?
   W: Help you! Do you think I work here?
   Q: What does Jack mean?
6. *M*: There's Bill on his motorcycle. Did he take it to the garage to be fixed?
   W: Don't be silly; that would have been a waste of money. It only had a flat tire.
   Q: What conclusion can be drawn from the woman's statement?
7. *W*: Are you coming with me to the museum?
   M: I already have my hands full with this report.
   Q: What does the man mean?
8. *M*: This train was supposed to get to Washington at 8 o'clock.
   W: 8 o'clock! But it's already eight thirty!
   Q: What does the woman mean?

9. ***W*:** Jerald Brown told me that Green and Company is going to publish his new novel.
***M*:** I had no idea he was such a talented writer.
***Q*:** What does the man conclude about Jerald Brown?

10. ***W*:** I heard on the radio that the storm is getting nearer.
***M*:** If the weatherman is as accurate as usual it will probably be sunny all day.
***Q*:** What do we learn from this conversation?

11. ***M*:** I'm going to ask my neighbours to turn the music down. I can't hear myself speak.
***W*:** Do you really think it makes any difference to them?
***Q*:** What does the woman imply?

12. ***W*:** Do you want me to explain those problems before your exam?
***M*:** What's the point? I don't understand a thing.
***Q*:** What does the man mean?

13. ***M*:** Well, I suppose I must take *Introduction to Engineering*.
***W*:** I'm afraid you must, but you needn't worry. It's only two hours per week.
***Q*:** What does the woman mean?

14. ***W*:** I thought you were going to drive carefully so you wouldn't get a traffic ticket.
***M*:** I was, but it didn't work out that way.
***Q*:** What can we assume about the man?

15. ***M*:** Jim has lots of good ideas. Do you think he'll be willing to come to this meeting?
***W*:** Oh, I think he'll be glad to come. What will be difficult is getting him to speak before a large crowd.
***Q*:** What does the woman imply about Jim?

Part Two Dialogue

I Want A Change

1. 1) F 2) F 3) T 4) T 5) T 6) T
2. 1) out of a job 2) bad news
3) the third time in five years 4) quit working
5) my own boss 6) a little nervous
7) health insurance 8) tired of being dependent
9) on their own 10) the younger generation

11) on a temporary basis
12) where they need him
13) the freedom he enjoys
14) employment agency
15) gave you more freedom
16) With your attitude and ability

Tapescript

Woman: I read that your company is downsizing again. What will that mean for your job?

Man: It means I'm out of a job. They have already given me a "pink slip".

Woman: That's bad news. This has happened to you before, hasn't it?

Man: Yes. This will be the third time in five years and I'm ready to call it quits.

Woman: What do you mean? You're going to quit working?

Man: No, I'll still be working, but not for a company. I'm going to be my own boss.

Woman: Doesn't that make you a little nervous? You won't have all the benefits that go with working for a company — no retirement, no health insurance.

Man: That is the bad part of it, but I am really tired of being dependent on the whims of big business. It seems that it hasn't been all that secure for me.

Woman: What will you do?

Man: I've had a couple of friends who have gone out on their own. They say it is the best thing that ever happened to them.

Woman: I know it is the secret dream of a lot of people to be their own boss, especially the younger generation.

Man: One of my friends just takes temporary jobs. Companies are looking for people with his skills, but only on a temporary basis. So he goes from one company to another, depending on where they need him. He's able to set his own working hours and he makes a lot more than he did when he was working full time. He really likes the freedom he enjoys.

Woman: What does he do when he doesn't have any jobs coming in?

Man: He goes to a temporary employment agency. It seems he always finds work and at double what he used to make.

Woman: I hope you find just the right thing for your skills. It would be nice to have a job that gave you more freedom.

Man: That's why I'm making the change. I want to be able to spend the extra time with my family.

Woman: Good luck! With your attitude and ability, I'm sure you'll do well.

Part Three Compound Dictation

Big Lesson from McDonald's

1) clownish
2) presence
3) lifestyle
4) valued
5) counter
6) energetic
7) restaurant
8) McDonald's crews undergo a Certificate in Food Retail training in some countries
9) Even the advertising agency employees working for McDonald's have to spend some time in the kitchen and behind the counter to learn "hands-on" about the business and the customers
10) Hopefully, what McDonald's has been doing about training will inspire other companies to be committed to their employees and community training—continuously and consistently

Tapescript

Almost every where you go around the world, you see the famous McDonald's "Golden arches" and the clownish figure of Ronald McDonald. Indeed, it has become a part of our lives.

The McDonald's presence in each market brings a new kind of lifestyle for kids, teenagers, families, and working people. The restaurant offers good quality and highly valued fast food. The people behind each McDonald's counter may be young or old, but most of them are enthusiastic, energetic, polite and efficient.

It must be the way McDonald's recruits and trains its employees that makes them shine over other restaurant workers.

McDonald's crews undergo a Certificate in Food Retail training in some countries, learning about customer service, food retailing, food preparation, hygiene standards, health and safety issues, security and other food-related issues.

All this training is done on the job. On top of that, McDonald's offers no-obligation scholarships to assist employees in their external education.

Even the advertising agency employees working for McDonald's have to spend some time in the kitchen and behind the counter to learn "hands-on" about the business and the customers.

Such training conditions the staff in the right attitudes — respect for customers and colleagues, and responsibility in doing a good job, no matter how menial it may seem. Hopefully, what McDonald's has been doing about training will inspire other companies to be committed to their employees and community training — continuously and consistently.

Part Four Passages

A. Management and Culture

1. 1) F 2) F 3) T 4) T 5) F
2. 1) The Westerners feel strongly about the individual's position.
   2) The bottom-up approach is used by management. In the Bottom-up approach the workers are involved in the decision. The company acts together as a unit, agreement between everyone is important.
   3) The Japanese use "you-to-you" approach. An understanding between the two people is the goal. Differences in opinion are not encouraged.
   4) The Western approach is, however, an "I to you" approach. Any differences in opinion are said clearly. This approach will create arguments.

Tapescript

Management is greatly influenced by culture. Both Japan and Western countries are developed countries. But the history and culture of Japan is very different from the history and culture of Western countries. These differences make their management styles very different from each other.

Three cultural differences between Japan and Western countries will be discussed. The first difference is in the employee's feelings towards the company. Let's begin with an example. How do children answer the question: "What does your father do?" In Western countries these are the probable answers: "My daddy is a truck driver," or "My daddy is a manager." The listener only knows a part of the answer. The truck driver's company or the manager's business are not known. On the other hand, in

Japan these children's probable answers to the same question would be: " My daddy works for Mitsubishi," or "My daddy works for Hitachi." Again the listener only knows a part of the answer. Is the child's father a driver or the president for Mitsubishi? The listener doesn't know. This example shows a basic difference. The Japanese feel strongly about the company; the Westerners feel strongly about the individual's position.

The second difference concerns the decision process. In Japan they use the bottom-up approach, the workers are involved in the decisions. The company acts together as a unit. Agreement among all the staff is important. On the contrary, decisions in Western countries are usually made top-down. They are made by the managers. Then the decisions are given to the workers.

Finally, the discussion approach is different between these two groups. The Japanese use a "you to you" approach. An understanding between the two people is the goal. Differences in opinion are not encouraged. The Western approach is, however, an "I to you" approach. Any differences in opinion are said clearly. This approach will create arguments.

Neither Japanese nor Western culture is particularly good or bad; they are different, and these cultural differences greatly influence the management style.

B. Entrepreneurial Process

1. 1) the computer operating system; the richest man
   2) delivers packages; within 24 hours; in1973; only 26; in a college term paper; 2 billion dollars; more than 25,000 people
   3) a 28-year-old housewife; a shopping center in her hometown; more than 200; in North America and Asia
2. 1) They started with a dream and worked very hard.
   2) They created companies that solve serious, important problems.
   3) They provide jobs for millions of people.
   4) And in general their contributions make life easier, more pleasant and more convenient for all of us.

Tapescript

Microsoft Corporation, Federal Express, and Mrs. Fields Cookies are well-established and famous companies all over the world. The people who started them are respectively Bill Gates, Frederick Smith and Bedd Fields. Bill Gates became famous when he developed the computer operating system called MS-DOS. Today he is the richest man in US. Federal Express, the company that delivers packages anywhere in the United States within 24 hours, was started in 1973 by a man named Frederick Smith. He was only 26 at the time. He had first suggested the ideas for his company in a college term paper. Today his company is worth about 2 billion dollars and employs more than 25,000 people. Bedd Fields was a 28-year-old housewife when she started her first chocolate chip cookie shop at a shopping center in her hometown. There are now more than 200 Mrs. Fields Cookie shops in North America and Asia. These three are famous examples of entrepreneurs.

Actually, as we all can see, entrepreneurs come from very different backgrounds. Some like Fred Smith and Bill are from rich families, but others are poor, some have a lot of education, but some, never finished college. But they do go through the same entrepreneurial process when they start their businesses.

Basically all of them follow the same six steps. First they identify a problem or a need; in other words, they see a need or problem that no one else sees. Second they think of a solution — what needs to be done to solve the problem or meet the need. Next, they prepare a business plan, which includes factors such as equipment, location, number of employees, financing, marketing, etc. This stage can take months or years. Fourth, they put together an entrepreneurial team — the people who will work with them to establish the business. In the fifth stage, they manufacture and test a small sample of the product or service and try to sell it to customers. This is called "test-marketing." And if customers like the product, entrepreneurs go on to the sixth stage: raising capital. "Capital" here means money. The entrepreneur has to find large amounts of money in order to produce and sell the product or service in large quantities.

Entrepreneurs like Bill Gates and the others are among the most respected people in the United States. They are regarded as heroes, and with good reasons. They started with a dream and worked very hard. They created companies that solve serious, important problems. They provide jobs for millions of people, and in general their contributions make life easier, more pleasant and more convenient for all of us.

Unit Four Arts

Part One Short Conversations

1. B 2. B 3. D 4. C 5. D 6. B 7. A 8. C
9. A 10. C 11. A 12. B 13. B 14. D 15. A

Tapescript

1. *M*: Can you give me a hand tomorrow? I want to rearrange some things in our spare room.
   W: Tomorrow is impossible, but I am free this weekend.
   Q: What does the man ask the woman to do?
2. *W*: I am sorry, sir. The train is somehow behind schedule. Take a seat and I'll tell you as soon as we know something definite.
   M: Thank you. I'll just sit here and read magazine in the meantime.
   Q: What can you conclude about the train from the conversation?
3 *W*: I need a car this weekend. But mine has broken down.
   M: I'm sorry to hear it. But you can always rent one if you have a license.
   Q: What does the man mean?
4. *M*: Please buy two packs of cigarettes for me while you are at the store.
   W: I am not going to any store. I am going to see aunt Mary. But I will get them for you at the gas station.
   Q: Where will the woman stop on her way?
5. *W*: Excuse me, sir! I am going to send this parcel to London. What's the postage for it?
   M: Let me see. It's one pound and fifty.
   Q: Who is the woman most probably speaking to?
6. *W*: Jack, I can't find Volume Ten. Could you check for me who borrowed it?
   M: Here it is on the upper shelf next to Volume Two.
   Q: Why can't the woman find the book?
7. *M*: Would you rather eat at home or go out tonight?
   W: I'd rather go out, but if you'd rather not go, I don't mind fixing supper at home.

Q: What does the woman want to do?

8. **W**: I simply don't know how to handle my naughty son.

   M: Why don't talk to Mike? He used to work with boys.

   Q: What do we learn about Mike from the conversation?

9. **M**: I'm worried about sending my son to college. Most college students are so wild nowadays.

   W: Only a few are. Most students are too busy studying to get into trouble.

   Q: What does the woman think of the man's remarks?

10. **M**: My radio doesn't work. What do you think I should do?

    W: Why don't you call Jimmy?

    Q: What does the woman mean?

11. **W**: Open wide. Now show me where it hurts.

    M: Here on the bottom, especially when I bite into something hot or cold.

    Q: Who is the woman?

12. **M**: Do you have a room with a private bath?

    W: Yes, sir. How about Room 201 on the second floor?

    Q: Where does this conversation most probably take place?

13. **M**: Mary, did you drop off the roll of film for developing?

    W: No, I got Susan to do it.

    Q: What happened to the roll of film?

14. **W**: Do you think you could give me a ride to the library tonight?

    M: I'd like to but I'm heading in the other direction. I'm meeting Jean tonight.

    Q: What will the man do that night?

15. **M**: Could you please explain the homework for Monday, Miss Smith?

    W: Certainly, read the next chapter in your textbook and come to class prepared to discuss what you've read.

    Q: What is the probable relationship between the two speakers?

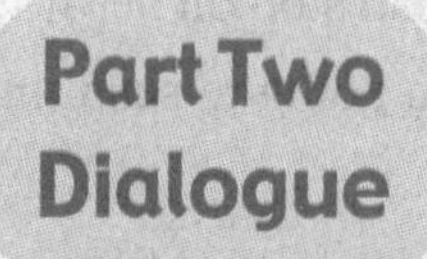

Part Two Dialogue

Have You Ever Heard of the Mona Lisa?

1. 1) Leonardo da Vinci.

   2) A famous painter from Holland in 1600s.

3) Collectors and investors.

4) How to paint abstract art.

2. 1) subjective
2) an authentic specimen
3) another famous painter
4) let alone their works
5) special subjects
6) extremely interested
7) the investment value
8) abstract enough

Tapescript

Woman: Have you ever heard of the Mona Lisa, Dick?

Man: Yeah, sure. It's one of the most famous paintings made by the Italian artist and inventor Leonardo da Vinci. Some people say that it is a picture of himself as a woman. Do you believe that?

Woman: That's hard to say because a great artist could do that. This is also why many copies were made.

Man: But really Anna, why would a man paint himself as a woman, or vice versa?

Woman: I don't know. If you ask me, I prefer him as a woman. Have you ever seen a Rembrandt painting?

Man: Art is so subjective. It is becoming very difficult to separate the difference between an authentic specimen and a fake one. Who's Rembrandt again?

Woman: He's another famous painter from Holland who did his most important work in the 1600s.

Man: I have a hard time remembering all of the great artists, let alone their works.

Woman: Most people have the same problem. Art is one of those special subjects.

Man: Yes, I agree. There are two kinds of people. The first, collectors, are extremely interested in all the different pieces and their details. The second, investors, have the extra money to purchase art for the investment value.

Woman: I'm still just an admirer of good art.

Man: I'd like to learn how to paint abstract art. That would be cool!

Woman: Just paint yourself. That should be abstract enough.

Part Three Compound Dictation

Silk-screening

1) frame
2) chemicals
3) plates
4) required
5) several
6) sharp
7) accurate
8) The artist prepares the fabric or paper by inserting it into the device that will hold it in place
9) When the artist pulls the ink across the screen, the parts of the silk that were not cut out by the chemicals resist the ink
10) By adding several layers of colors on top of each other, it is possible to produce images that appear to be almost photographic

Tapescript

Silk-screening is the art of producing pictures by printing on specially prepared silk screens. After a thin piece of silk has been tacked onto a special frame, the picture is cut through the silk by brushing in a layer of chemicals that weaken certain areas of the silk. A series of plates needs to be made for each different layer of color that will be required in the final product. It is possible to use several colors on one screen, but if you desire sharp, clean lines, it is best to use one color per screen.

When the screens have been cut, it is important that some method be used to keep them in an accurate position. If one of the screens is out of place, the printing won't look right. The artist prepares the fabric or paper by inserting it into the device that will hold it in place. The first screen is applied, and the color is scraped across the screen with a smooth piece of wood or rubber. This process is known as "pulling". When the artist pulls the ink across the screen, the parts of the silk that were not cut out by the chemicals resist the ink. The parts which were cut by the chemicals allow the ink to pass through and create the image. By adding several layers of colors on top of each other, it is possible to produce images that appear to be almost photographic.

Part Four
Passages

A. The Shaker Furniture

1. 1) B 2) A 3) C 4) B
2. 1) Solidly constructed. 2) Lightweight.
   3) Very simple. 4) Useful.
   5) Durable.

Tapescript

Settlers originally came to the American continent so they could practice their religion as they wished, free from the religious persecution of that era. One of these religious groups that settled in the U.S. was the Shakers. The Shakers prospered in the first half of the nineteenth century and, at their height, totaled about 6000 members. They are, however, not known for their religion, but for the furniture they make during the first half of the nineteenth century. This was perhaps their greatest accomplishment. The furniture was solidly constructed, yet lightweight at the same time. The designs were also very simple because anything elaborate was not allowed, according to their religious principles. The Shakers believed that any decoration would insult or challenge their God, so they created furniture unique in its amazingly simple designs.

In the nineteenth century, their furniture was very popular because it was useful and durable. In the twentieth, people mostly value it for its beauty, in addition to its other characteristics. Museums and collectors praise the furniture as one of the best of examples of American design. Currently, only twelve aged Shakers remain, and none of them constructs furniture any longer. Hence, Shaker tables, chairs, cabinets, and other pieces are valuable collectors' items because they are now very rare. Although the furniture may no longer be produced, the Shakers and their furniture will forever remain an important chapter in the art design of the United States. They are good examples of true American design.

B. Trafalgar Square

1. 1) T 2) T 3) F 4) F 5) F

2. 1) a good site; the Spanish and French navies
   2) the height of the column
   3) over £2 million; a safe height above his creditors
   4) feed the pigeons; demonstrations and political rallies
   5) a direct telephone link; particularly full or busy

Tapescript

Trafalgar Square was built before any specific plans to commemorate Nelson's naval victory in 1805 had been made. Only an initialed letter to *The Times* newspaper resulted in the building of the 170-foot (52 meters) column. The unknown letter writer suggested that the square was a good site to honor Nelson's victory against the Spanish and French navies. The column was designed by William Railton and was built between 1829 and 1842. The 17-foot (5.3 meters) high statue was sculpted by E.H. Balley. It was criticized because people thought it was too simple. They forgot that no-one would be able to see Nelson's face!

People also criticized the height of the column, which they said spoilt the Whitehall view. One reason why it was so high was because people wanted it to rise above the Duke of York's a 124-foot (37.8 meters) column in nearby Waterloo Place. A high column was built for him for a very good reason. The Duke of York died with debts of over £2 million and so it was suggested that he should be a safe height above his creditors.

In Trafalgar Square today, many tourists feed the pigeons and British people gather there for demonstrations and political rallies. On New Year's Eve, they often sing and dance in the fountains. Very few notice the small police station in the South-East corner. This is inside the hollow column of one of the lamps and if you are lucky, you might see a policeman stepping into it. This is the smallest police station in England and is just large enough for two policemen or a policeman and a policewoman. They have a direct telephone link with New Scotland Yard near Victoria Station and quietly keep an eye on Trafalgar Square when it is particularly full or busy.

Unit Five Man and Nature

Part One Short Conversations

1. C 2. A 3. D 4. C 5. D 6. D 7. B 8. B
9. A 10. A 11. C 12. C 13. C 14. D 15. A

Tapescript

1. ***W***: I'm sorry I caused your uncle so much trouble.
   M: Don't worry about it. He is the sort of man who is never happy unless he has something to complain about.
   Q: What does the man mean?
2. ***W***: Try to cut out smoking. That's the first thing you should do if you are worried about your health.
   M: That's a lot easier said than done.
   Q: What does the man mean?
3. ***M***: I wonder if Ann will really come at 7. She said she would. Look at the time now.
   W: Don't worry. Her word is as good as gold.
   Q: What does the woman mean?
4. ***W***: The service in this restaurant is really terrible.
   M: Right. It's high time they got rid of half of the staff here, if you ask me.
   Q: What conclusion can you draw from the conversation.
5. ***M***: Could I borrow your car for just one night?
   W: That's out of the question.
   Q: What does the woman mean?
6. ***M***: I don't know why Mr. William's phone number isn't listed on the yellow pages.
   W: But it is.
   Q: What does the woman say about Mr. Williams number?
7. ***M***: Did you have a good time yesterday? I heard there was a heavy rain.
   W: Yeh. We enjoyed ourselves very much except for the bad weather in the end. Jane would have been caught in the rain if she had come back on foot.

Q: What do we know about Jane?

8. *W*: If I were you, I'd like to go by air instead of by coach.

   M: But flying makes me so nervous.

   Q: What does the man prefer to do?

9. *W*: Jane told me that she was leaving for Boston. I'll certainly be sorry to see her go.

   M: Oh, she always says that! I wouldn't buy her a going-away present if I were you.

   Q: What does the man think Jane will do?

10. *M*: Do you think we should put an ad in the newspaper for the lost car?

    W: By all means.

    Q: What does the woman mean?

11. *W*: Are there any other papers missing besides the credit card?

    M: You bet there are! Passport, checkbook, credit cards, the whole works!

    Q: What can you infer from the conversation?

12. *M*: How were their talks going? Have they reached an agreement?

    W: They only seemed to have agreed to set another date for further talks.

    Q: What can we infer from the conversation?

13. *W*: There was a new quiz show on television last night, but we were just sitting down to dinner when it came on.

    M: I watched it and it was great! The first four contestants won only small prizes, but the fifth left with a new luxury car.

    Q: What happened last night?

14. *M*: Why were you so strongly opposed to your son skipping a grade in school?

    W: There's too much pressure and competition in our society. Of course, I want my son to succeed, but I want him to enjoy his childhood as well. There's more to life than having a million-dollar-a-year job.

    Q: What does the lady's opinion indicate?

15. *W*: I wish I hadn't thrown away that list of books.

    M: I thought you might, need it later on, so I took it from the waste paper basket. It's right here in my pocket book.

    Q: What do we learn about the list?

Part Two Dialogue

What Happens to the Baby Seals?

1. 1) A 2) A 3) B 4) A
2. 1) in a hurry 2) protesting
   3) lovely wild fox furs 4) for instance
   5) Out on the ice 6) all the fish
   7) the fur industry 8) covered in blood
   9) sign your petition 10) give a donation
   11) go to the sales 12) plastic ones

Tapescript

Man: Madam, can I have a word with you?

Woman: Well ... er ... I'm in a hurry. I'm going to the sales of the fur coats.

Man: It won't take a moment.

Woman: OK.

Man: Do you know why we're protesting outside this store?

Woman: Oh, it's something to do with the fur coats, isn't it? They've got some lovely wild fox furs.

Man: Do you know how many animals are killed to make one coat? Do you know what happens to baby seals for instance?

Woman: Well, they're put to death painlessly, aren't they?

Man: They're clubbed to death. Out on the ice. They're taken from their mothers, chased across the ice, and then beaten to death with clubs.

Woman: They have to be controlled. If they aren't controlled, they eat all the fish. They have to be killed.

Man: They don't have to be killed, you know. It's only the fur industry that says that. Nature has its own way of control. Look at the picture of that poor little seal. It's all covered in blood.

Woman: Oh, it's horrible!

Man: That's how the seals are killed. That's the evidence.

Woman: Here I'll sign your petition.

Man: Perhaps you'd like to give a donation to "Friends of the Earth"? You can stop the world's wildlife from disappearing.

Woman: Yes. I think I will. But I'd still like to go to the sales.

Man: One day there won't be any wild animals left in the world. You'll just have plastic ones in Disneyland.

Part Three Compound Dictation

The Balance of Nature

1) exist
2) joined
3) natural
4) certainly
5) forests
6) insects
7) widespread
8) The throwing of waste products into the oceans damages life in the sea
9) Man is very clever at changing the world around him to satisfy his immediate needs
10) Man may well, in his attempt to be too ambitious, destroy himself

Tapescript

It is only during the last few years that man has become generally aware that in the world of nature a most delicate balance exists between all forms of life. No living things can exist by itself: it is part of a system in which all forms of life are joined together. If we change one part of the natural order, this will in its turn almost certainly bring about changes in some other part.

The cutting down of forests reduces the supply of oxygen. The killing of weeds and insects by chemicals leads to the widespread poisoning of animals and birds. The throwing of waste products into the oceans damages life in the sea, while exhaust fumes change the chemical balance of the atmosphere and shut out some of the sun's essential life-giving rays.

And so we could go on, adding more examples, until in despair we might feel like giving up the struggle to control and keep within limits these harmful human activities. Man is very clever at changing the world around him to satisfy his immediate needs, but he is not so clever at looking far ahead, or at thinking about what the future results of his actions might be. Man may well, in his attempt to be too ambitious, destroy himself.

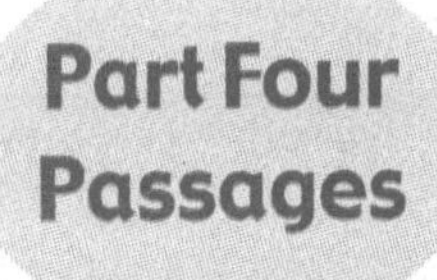

Part Four Passages

A. Outdoor Plants Move Inside

1. 1) A 2) C 3) D 4) C
2. 1) a. The modern indoor environment can be an ideal setting for a wide variety of outdoor plants.
   b. Modern use of windows has made exotic outdoor plants more practical.
   2) a. Orchid
   b. Vines

Tapescript

For years, it's been assumed that the indoor environment limits the variety of plants that people are exposed to. Lately, however, plants that are usually only grown outdoors have found their way into indoor spaces. There are a few simple reasons why this is.

The modern indoor environment can be an ideal setting for a wide variety of outdoor plants. Plants that ordinarily cannot grow in colder outdoor climates can find protection from the cold indoors, where temperatures are easily controlled. Plants that used to be found outside, such as trees, have become more and more popular as decorations inside houses. Orchids, which were once only found in tropical environments, have begun to thrive in indoor setting. A large number of smaller plants have also found their way into homes.

One aspect of the modern home that has made exotic outdoor plants more practical is the modern use of windows. In the past windows were used less frequently in buildings than they are today. It is partly because of the ability of large windows to admit large amounts of sunlight and keep the heat in at the same time that many outdoor plants have been able to make their move inside.

It is true that most of the plants that have been successful in moving indoors have been small. Some of the best adapted varieties are the vines. Many vines that are parasitic in natural surroundings make excellent decorations where other plants prove difficult to grow. Although some trees can be grown indoors, it is unlikely the larger varieties can be used. Unfortunately, most homes just don't have the space to grow a redwood tree.

B. World's Rivers Running Dry

1. 1) T 2) F 3) T 4) T 5) T
2. 1) two-thirds; one-quarter; 9%–10%
   2) building large dams; more than 5,000; 38,000
   3) tripled in the last 45 years

Tapescript

Some of the world's mightiest rivers never reach the sea. They've been diverted and siphoned off to grow cotton and lettuce, to fill bathtubs and swimming pools, to turn the turbines of power plants, to cool the wheels of industry.

Unfortunately, when planners were dividing up the river's resources, the rivers themselves didn't have anybody fighting for their right to be a river. So the diversion of the rivers to meet man's needs has greatly changed the ecology and habitat for fish and birds and other wildlife. Or simply erased it. Today many of the world's majestic rivers are drying up, many great mountain-born torrents have been reduced to a trickle.

What happened was a growing population and a need to bathe and feed them.

Of the world's total water demand, about two-thirds is for agriculture and another one-quarter goes for industrial use. The 9%–10% remaining quenches thirsts in cities and towns.

In Arizona, the United States, the Salt and Gila rivers used to join west of Phoenix. Today they dry up east of the city as thirsty farms divert their water. In the Middle East, the Jordan River is so overused that the lower stretches are no more than "a salty trickle".

In an effort to tame and use the rivers' flow, governments began building large dams. There were more than 5,000 large dams in 1950. There are 38,000 today. The world's dams hold about 15 percent of the planet's renewable water supply. In addition, there are thousands of miles of canals sucking water out of reservoirs and lakes to take it to where people demand it.

In the last 45 years, the demand for water has tripled.

There are some innovative schemes being born around the world to rescue some of the globe's important rivers. Agriculturally, drip irrigation lines or low-pressure sprinklers can reduce water's evaporation. Scheduling irrigation to match a crop's thirst can save tons of water. But there is probably no effective incentive to save water other than raising the cost of water.

Unit Six Social Welfare

Part One Short Conversations

1. D 2. D 3. C 4. C 5. D 6. D 7. B 8. C
9. B 10. D 11. A 12. A 13. D 14. A 15. A

Tapescript

1. ***M***: I feel we really need to buy a new car, but I don't see how we can possibly afford one right now.
   W: If only we hadn't spent so much money on our holiday this year.
   Q: What can we learn from the conversation?
2. ***M***: It doesn't make any sense to go home for the spring holiday now.
   W: That's right. Especially since you'll be graduating in May.
   Q: What can we learn from the conversation?
3. ***W***: Do you think you could have this skirt ready by Thursday morning?
   M: I'm sorry. I couldn't possibly get it done by then. Friday afternoon would be the earliest that you could have it.
   Q: What is the man's probable occupation?
4. ***W***: John must have been joking when he said that he was going to quit his job.
   M: Don't be so sure. He told me that he was trying to sell his house.
   Q: What does the man mean?
5. ***M***: Sorry to bother you, Mrs. Smith, but I'd like to ask you some questions.
   W: I'm never too busy to help a neighbor, Mr. Henderson. What would you like to know?
   Q: What can we infer from this conversation?
6. ***W***: Look at those colorful birds over there. I think you can teach them to talk.
   M: Yes. But look at the price tag on them!
   Q: What does the woman imply?
7. ***M***: Everyone hides in the next room and when Allen comes in, jumps out all at once.
   W: Maybe turning on a few lights will make her less suspicious.

Q: What are they probably doing?

8. *W*: The hot water is running in my house. I can't turn it off.
   M: Don't worry, Madam. Leave your address and I'll call Mr. Purnell immediately.
   Q: Who is Mr. Purnell?

9. *W*: Tony said he could lend me some money to buy the house.
   M: Tony always means what he says.
   Q: What does the man mean?

10. *W*: Should I make an appointment to see you again, Mr. Trott?
    M: I'm not sure if that is necessary, but you might call me on Friday morning. I'll be out of town Wednesday and Thursday.
    Q: When does this conversation most probably take place?

11. *M*: Just look at this newspaper. Nothing but murder, death, war. Do you still believe people are basically good in the modern times?
    W: Of course. Newspapers hardly ever report the stories about peace and generosity. They aren't news.
    Q: What is the woman's attitude about people?

12. *M*: I have never seen you have such confidence half an hour before an exam.
    W: It's more than confidence. Right now I feel that if I get less than an A, it'll be the exam's fault not mine.
    Q: What's the woman's attitude towards the examination?

13. *W*: Since you are a man, what made you decide to become a teacher?
    M: My father says, "Get your teaching degree and no matter what happens, you will always have something to fall back on."
    Q: What advice did the man receive and from whom?

14. *M*: It doesn't make any sense to copy so many questions before the final examination. They are unlikely to appear on the exam paper at all.
    W: That sounds all right, especially since these questions are somewhat too easy for us.
    Q: On what do the two agree?

15. *W*: Frank is always complaining about his job.
    M: Maybe if you are tired of waiting on tables, you'd see what it's like.
    Q: What does the man mean?

Part Two Dialogue

Is the United States A Welfare State?

1. 1) B 2) C 3) C 4) B 5) B
2. 1) Social stratification refers to divided social classes that have varying degrees of access to the rewards the society offers.
   2) Blue Cross is a not-for-profit insurance program that pays patients' hospital bills.
   3) Blue Shield is also a not-for-profit insurance program that covers doctors' fees for medical or surgical expenses inside the hospitals.
   4) Medicare is a program designed to cover some of the medical expenses of people over the age of sixty-five.
   5) Medicaid is a program designed to cover the medical expenses of people with very low income.

Tapescript

Student: Professor Li, you told us a lot about the welfare system in Britain. But is the United States a welfare state?

Professor: Mm ... To a large extent, it's not. First of all, the United States doesn't have a national health-insurance program or some similar means of making health care freely available to all who need it.

Student: But the United States is a country of wealth, isn't it?

Professor: Yes. That's true. But the social stratification is also obvious in the US.

Student: What do you mean by "social stratification"?

Professor: It means that the American society is divided into social classes that have varying degrees of access to the rewards the society offers. The richest fifth of American individuals and families owns more than three quarters of the wealth in the United States, whereas the lowest fifth owns only 0.2 percent of the wealth.

Student: So there exists uneven distribution of wealth between the rich and the poor in the US. What kind of medical treatment can the poor obtain then?

Professor: Unlike the rich who can afford to enjoy the services of highly paid specialists, the poor have to attend municipal clinics and hospitals, often waiting for hours or days for appointment. They are likely to be seen by different doctors on each visit. If they are hospitalized, they may be under the care of the poorly trained doctors.

Student: And what is the primary goal of American health-care system?

Professor: The primary goal is to make money. In the US, medical care is regarded as a private business, based on the principle that the kind of care you receive depends on how much money you are willing or able to spend.

Student: Are there any special medical programs in the United States then?

Professor: Yes. There are Blue Cross, Blue Shield as well as Medicare and Medicaid programs in the US.

Student: I have only heard of Red Cross. What does Blue Cross mean? And what are Blue Shield and...?

Professor: Blue Cross is a not-for-profit insurance program that pays patients' hospital bills. Blue Shield is also a not-for-profit insurance program that covers doctors' fees for medical and surgical expenses inside the hospitals. But the primary purpose of the "Blues" is not to save money by keeping bills down; rather, it is to ensure that hospital bills, however high they may be, get paid. Medicare is a program designed to cover some of the medical expenses of people over the age of sixty-five while Medicaid is designed to cover the medical expenses of people with very low income.

Student: So the American poor and old can share some of the profits after all.

Professor: Yes. You are right.

Student: Thanks a lot for your help, Professor Li.

Professor: You're always welcome.

Part Three Compound Dictation

Old People in Britain

1) quarter
2) poverty
3) range
4) divorced
5) socially
6) mentally
7) discrimination

8) Older people are a valuable resource to our society and yet are very often socially excluded from everyday activities and services

9) This valuable resource should be "tapped" by government, recognized and respected by society

10) to have access to educational and training opportunities to learn new skills and gain new knowledge

Tapescript

According to the British government figures, more than half of the nation's single pensioners have net incomes of less than £90 a week. A quarter of couples have net incomes of less than £135 a week. While to achieve an "acceptable" standard of living for older people and to avoid poverty, the figures, according to a research commissioned by Age Concern England, range from £99 to £125 a week for single people and from £149 to £184 for couples.

Coupled with low net incomes is the health needs of older people. The health needs of older people cannot be divorced from their level of income and housing conditions. If older people are poor, ill-housed and socially excluded, they are more likely to become physically and mentally ill. In addition, recent research undertaken by Age Concern England identified the existence of age discrimination within NHS (National Health Service).

Older people are a valuable resource to our society and yet are very often socially excluded from everyday activities and services. As individual citizens they have the right to equality of opportunity to an adequate income and services to enable them to lead a fulfilling and enjoyable life.

Older people have a wealth of knowledge and experience that can be utilized to the benefit of society as a whole. This valuable resource should be "tapped" by government, recognized and respected by society.

Opportunities should be made available to people aged 50 and over to continue in paid employment if this is what they wish to do; and to have access to educational and training opportunities to learn new skills and gain new knowledge.

Part Four
Passages

A. Why Is Britain Dubbed as A Welfare State?

1. 1) A 2) D 3) B
2. 1) An employed British citizen must contribute to the National Insurance and Health Schemes.
   2) An employer must also contribute for his employees.
   3) The Government.
   4) In 1968.

Tapescript

Britain is usually dubbed as the welfare state because first it ensures, as far as it can, that nobody be without the means for the minimum necessities of life as the result of unemployment, old age, sickness or over-large families. Then the system of National Insurance pays out benefits to people who are unemployed, or unable to earn because they are old or sick. Also, free or nearly free medical and dental care is provided for everyone under the National Health Service. At the same time supplementary benefits are provided for people who live below the minimum standard.

The system of National Insurance requires every British citizen who is employed (or self-employed) be obliged to pay a weekly contribution to the National Insurance and Health Schemes. An employer also makes a contribution for his employees, and the Government, too, pays a certain amount. This plan was brought into being first in 1948 and was reorganized in 1968.

The National Health Service is financed partly by weekly contributions by people who are working, but mainly by payments by the state out of general taxation. Everyone can register with a doctor without having to pay for the doctor's services, although he has to pay a small charge (£5) for medicines. The doctor, may, if necessary, send a patient to a specialist, or to a hospital. In both cases treatment will be given without any fee being payable. However, many people who have enough money still prefer to be private patients.

It is true that some people who are entitled to the benefits still live in poverty. It's because they are too proud to receive the benefits, or do not understand the system of the welfare state, or do not know how to apply.

B. A Generous Gift

1. 1) A 2) C 3) D 4) C
2. 1) as well as singers; raise money
   2) neither rich nor poor; perform some charities
   3) collecting money; gave her a painting; increased the value

Tapescript

In this highly competitive world, there are always people who are in the disadvantage. These are the old, the sick and the parentless. On the other hand, however, there are also always people who are kind and sympathetic. Rich people often donate money to public welfare projects. Actors and actresses as well as singers often give benefit performances to raise money for the poor and the needy. People, who are neither rich nor poor but with any performing skills and with a kind heart, also take part by offering to perform some charities. A woman in the following story is just one of them.

Once a woman was collecting money for a church charity. The money she collected was going to be given to poor children who had no parents to take care of them.

She went from apartment to apartment and from house to house. She knocked on doors and asked for money.

She always said the same thing.

"Good morning, I'm collecting for a church charity. Please give generously. We need $5,000." Then she held out a collecting box. Most people put a few coins in the box.

An artist lived in one of the apartments. He opened the door to her.

"Good morning," she said. "I'm collecting for a church charity. Please give generously. We need $5,000."

The artist thought for a moment, then he said, "I'm sorry, but I don't have any money. However, I'll give you a painting. It's worth $400."

The woman thanked the artist and took the painting away.

A week later she called on him again.

"I'm sorry to trouble you again," she said, "but we still need more money. I need another $100. Can you help?"

"Of course," the artist said, "I'll increase the value of my painting to $500."

Unit Seven Distance Learning

Part One Short Conversations

1. A 2. A 3. B 4. B 5. B 6. C 7. B 8. D
9. A 10. D 11. A 12. B 13. D 14. D 15. A

Tapescript

1. *M*: Did you go dancing with Tom last night? He is a good dancer, isn't he?
   W: All right. I'm fed up with him.
   Q: What's the woman's attitude to Tom?
2. *W*: Where shall I pay for the food stuffs?
   M: At the checkout counter near the main entrance. It's over there, see it?
   Q: Where does the woman want to go?
3 *M*: I want to have this shirt washed and this suit dry cleaned. When can I have them back please?
   W: Oh, I'll send them to your home as soon as I've got them done.
   Q: Where does the conversation take place?
4. *W*: I went to a modern art exhibition yesterday. It's really abstract. Do you like modern art?
   M: I certainly do, yet not so much as the classical art.
   Q: What kind of art does the man prefer?
5. *W*: Miss Green is a very well-known film star, and John is famous too.
   M: Do you really think so? I believe that Austen is more famous than both of them and John is the last one I'd regard as famous.
   Q: Whom does the man consider the least famous?
6. *M*: Let me get you some tea or coffee, but what would you prefer?
   W: Just a glass of soda will be OK.
   Q: What does the woman want to have?
7. *M*: If you're introduced to a friend's wife, what would you do?
   W: Ah, if I call that friend by his first name, and then meet his wife, I'll probably start out calling his wife "Mrs".

Q: What's the relationship between the two speakers?

8. *W*: I'm really looking forward to the next Olympic Games.

   M: Me, too. The 1980 Olympics were so disappointing with so many countries withdrawing and refusing to compete in Russia.

   Q: Why is the man particularly looking forward to the next Olympic Games?

9. *M*: What happened to you? You're so late.

   W: My car broke down on the highway, and I had to walk.

   Q: Why did the woman have to walk?

10. *M*: This motorcycle cost $1,000. I think it's too expensive.

    W: You shouldn't have felt so. Motorcycles of the same type are more expensive in other shops.

    Q: How did the woman feel about the motorcycle the man bought?

11. *M*: The special plane will land at 8:15 a.m., Beijing time.

    W: It's early. Let's go and have a drink.

    Q: When will the special plane land?

12. *W*: The sales of industrial products have multiplied eight times since liberation.

    M: That's true.

    Q: Which of the following is true?

13. *M*: Hello! Is this triple eight double zero four two?

    W: Yes. Who is speaking?

    Q: What is the telephone number?

14. *M*: There are 65 people for the meeting.

    W: I know, but thirteen have phoned to ask for leave.

    Q: How many people will turn up for the meeting?

15. *W*: What time does the plane take off?

    M: Not until 9:15, but I want to get to the airport by 8:30.

    Q: How long will the man wait at the airport?

Part Two Dialogue

I Will Try It Out

1. 1) B 2) D 3) A 4) D 5) C
2. 1) It allows more flexibility in students' schedules.

2) It limits interaction among students.

3) After each part of the series, students have to make phone contacts with their professor and other students about their ideas. They will meet on campus three times for reviews and exams.

Tapescript

M: *Mike* ***L***: *Linda*

M: Hi, Linda.

L: Hi, Mike. You look smart today.

M: Thank you. I saw you at registration yesterday. I sailed right through. But you were standing in a line.

L: Yeah, I waited an hour to sign up for a distance learning cause.

M: Distance learning? Never heard of it.

L: Well, it's new this semester. It's only open to psychology majors. But I believe it'll catch on elsewhere. Yesterday over a hundred students signed up.

M: Well, what is it?

L: It's an experimental course. I registered for Child Psychology. All I got to do is watch a twelve-week series of television lessons. The department shows them several different times a day and in several different locations.

M: Don't you ever have to meet with your professor?

L: Yeah. After each part of the series, I have to talk to her and the other students on the phone, you know, about our ideas. Then we'll meet on campus three times for reviews and exams.

M: It sounds pretty non-traditional to me. But I guess it makes sense considering how many students have jobs. It must really help with their schedules. Not to mention how it'll cut down on traffic.

L: You know, last year my department did a survey and they found that 80% of all psychology majors were employed. That's why they came up with the program. Look, I'll be working three days a week next semester and it was either cut back on my classes or try this out.

M: The only thing is, doesn't it seem impersonal though? I mean, I miss having class discussions and hearing what other people think.

L: Well, I guess that's why phone contacts are important. Anyway, it's an experiment. Maybe I'll end up hating it.

Part Three Compound Dictation

Distance Education in Britain

1) interact
2) artificial
3) correspondence
4) specifically
5) evaluates
6) efficient
7) available
8) Nearly every country in the world makes use of distance education programs in its education system
9) More than 20 other countries have national open universities in which all instruction is provided by distance education methods
10) Many businesses use distance education programs to train employees or to help them update skills or knowledge. Employees may take such programs in the workplace or at home in their spare time

Tapescript

Distance education refers to methods of instruction that utilize different communications technologies to carry teaching to learners in different places. Distance education programs enable learners and teachers to interact with each other by means of computers, artificial satellites, telephones, radio or television broadcasting, or other technologies. Instruction conducted through the mail is often referred to as correspondence education, although many educators simply consider this the ancestor of distance education. Distance education is also sometimes called distance learning. While distance learning can refer to either formal or informal learning experiences, distance education refers specifically to formal instruction conducted at a distance by a teacher who plans, guides, and evaluates the learning process. As new communications technologies become more efficient and more widely available, increasing numbers of elementary schools, secondary schools, universities, and businesses offer distance education programs.

In Britain, from elementary schools to graduate schools, people have always focused much of their attention on formal education. At the same time, however, they have always maintained informal channels for learning well into adulthood, whether in the form of Bible classes, library programs, museum exhibitions, or other group activities. Nearly every country in the world makes use of distance education programs in its education system. Britain's nationally supported Open University, based in Milton Keynes, Buckinghamshire, England, has one of the best-known programs. A vast majority of the school's 133,000 students receive instruction entirely at a distance. More than 20 other countries have national open universities in which all instruction is provided by distance education methods. This method of education can be especially valuable in developing countries. By reaching a large number of students with relatively few teachers, it provides a cost-effective way of using limited academic resources. Many businesses use distance education programs to train employees or to help them update skills or knowledge. Employees may take such programs in the workplace or at home in their spare time.

Part Four Passages

A. History of Distance Education

1. 1) F 2) T 3) F 4) F 5) F 6) T 7) T

2.

When	What New Media Used in Distance Education
mid-19th century	postal system
in the 1920s	radio
in the 1940s	television
in the early 1900s	long-distance telephone systems
in the 1980s and 1990s	teleconferencing technologies
in the 1980s and 1990s	computer-network communications

Tapescript

Distance education traces its origins to mid-19th century Europe and the United States. The pioneers of distance education used the best technology of their day, the postal system, to open educational opportunities to people who wanted to learn but were not able to attend conventional schools. People who most benefited from such correspondence education included those with physical disabilities, women who were not allowed to enroll in educational institutions open only to men, people who had jobs during normal school hours, and those who lived in remote regions where schools did not exist.

The invention of educational radio in the 1920s and television in the 1940s created important new forms of communication for use in distance education. Educators used these new technologies to broadcast educational programs to millions of learners, thus extending learning opportunities beyond the walls of conventional teaching institutions.

The development of reliable long-distance telephone systems in the early 1900s also increased the capacity of distance educators to reach new student populations. But telephone systems never played a prominent role in education until the introduction of new teleconferencing technologies in the 1980s and 1990s. Teleconferencing systems made it possible for teachers to talk with, hear, and see their students in real time, that is, with no delays in the transmissions, even if they were located across the country or around the world.

Distance education increasingly uses combinations of different communications technologies to enhance the abilities of teachers and students to communicate with each other. With the spread of computer-network communications in the 1980s and 1990s, large numbers of people gained access to computers linked to telephone lines, allowing teachers and students to communicate in conferences via computers. Distance education also makes use of computer conferencing on the World Wide Web, where teachers and students present text, pictures, audio, and occasionally video. A conferencing method known as one-way video/two-way audio uses television pictures that are transmitted to particular sites, where people can reply to the broadcasters with a telephone call-in system. Television pictures can also be transmitted in two directions simultaneously through telephone lines, so that teachers and students in one place can see and hear teachers and students in other places. This is called video-conferencing.

B. IT and Language Learning

1. 1) F 2) T 3) T 4) F 5) F 6) T 7) F 8) T
2. 1) D 2) C 3) A 4) A

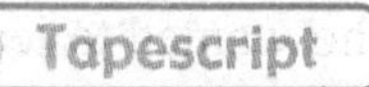

Nowadays, IT, the short form for information technology, and language learning are closely related. Before the arrival of multimedia, the future of computer-assisted language learning (the short form is CALL) was by no means assured. But today, no one doubts that CALL is here to stay. Nearly every institution in the UK has some sort of IT center, even if it consists of only a couple of PCs and some supermarket software.

This is hardly surprising, given the growth of new technology and the necessity of being computer literate. But there are additional, and more important reasons why IT and language learning should, and do, work so well together.

The first is multimedia's motivating influence on learners. Before computers came into widespread use, students were forced to battle with ponderous textbooks — no wonder that motivating learners was a problem. The passage to fluency was made easier with the arrival of authentic materials, which students read both for recreation and language purposes.

Second, multimedia seem to be the only medium that is broad enough to motivate students of any age. Children as young as three years old "who have never used a computer before take to multimedia like ducks to water. They are constantly captivated by pictures, sound and texts, combined with surprise". For older learners, it is the creative potential of CALL that really helps language acquisition.

Finally, the latest innovation in CALL is using the Internet in the classroom. It serves as a basis for language practice, where, for instance, they answer questions relating to information which is found on the Net. It is widely used for research support as well, particularly by students preparing essays and assignments. Students are also given the opportunity to create their own pages on the Net.

Unit Eight Famous Speeches

Part One Short Conversations

1. D 2. B 3. A 4. C 5. B 6. D 7. B 8. B
9. D 10. A 11. A 12. D 13. A 14. C 15. C

Tapescript

1. ***W***: Do you like this part of the country?
   M: Yes, it's very interesting. I like the climate. It's a lot like where I come from.
   Q: Why does he like the climate in this part of the country?
2. ***M***: Why don't you come with me to a big city? Maybe we can have a very comfortable life there.
   W: I was born here, my elderly parents here love me so deeply and I love living here.
   Q: What did the woman dislike?
3. ***W***: There is a limit of three books for each person. Do you still want to have them?
   M: Fine, thanks. I'll be certain to return them on time.
   Q: Where did the conversation take place?
4. ***M***: I live in a narrow room. It's rather dark and not so well-furnished.
   W: My living quarter is as good as yours.
   Q: What's true among the following?
5. ***M***: Is it still raining outside?
   W: No, but the wind is still blowing a bit.
   Q: What can be concluded from this conversation?
6. ***M***: I thought Francie and Mike were getting married in June.
   W: No , that's when his cousin's wedding is. They're getting married the following month.
   Q: When are Francie and Mike getting married?
7. ***W***: Don't take too long at the snack bar. It's a quarter past 12.
   M: It's OK. We have 45 minutes before the plane leaves.
   Q: What time is their departure scheduled?

8. ***M***: What about going to my hometown to have a good summer holiday?

W: Oh, wonderful, and I'll see the beautiful hills again.

Q: If the man's offer is accepted, where will the two go in summer?

9. ***M***: Hello, Switchboard, can I have a line, please?

W: Sorry, they are all engaged. Will you hold on?

Q: What do you think is the woman's profession?

10. ***W***: Open wide. Now show me where it hurts.

M: Here on the bottom, especially when I bite into something hot or cold.

Q: Who is the woman?

11. ***M***: The hall is big enough to hold hundreds of people.

W: That's a good place for a meeting.

Q: How many people can the hall hold?

12. ***M***: I'd like to withdraw $15 from my deposit account.

W: You have $125 left then.

Q: How much is there in the original deposit account?

13. ***W***: Do you want dollars or pounds?

M: I want pounds. Two tens and one five, please.

Q: How much money does the man want?

14. ***M***: Will Dr. Black be able to see me at nine fifteen tomorrow?

W: Sorry, but he's fully occupied till eleven. Would ten to one be convenient?

Q: When will Dr. Black be free?

15. ***M***: Do you know when this accident happened?

W: Yes, on the morning of the 30th of Dec., 1906.

Q: When did this accident happen?

Part Two Dialogue

Why, Mom, You Are Weeping?

1. 1) smuggle opium 2) a kind of poison
3) several years before that 4) a national hero
5) burnt it in Canton 6) launched a war of aggression
7) invaded our China 8) China ceded Hong Kong to Britain

Tapescript

Dongdong: Why, Mom, you are weeping? What makes you so sad?

Mother: No, I don't feel sad at all. I'm extremely excited. Listen, "Five hours from now the Union flag will be lowered and the flag of China will fly over Hong Kong."

Dongdong: What's the difference?

Mother: The return of Hong Kong, my boy. I'm thrilled.

Dongdong: Why does "the return of Hong Kong" make you so thrilled? Ah, I see. That's it.

Mother: What?

Dongdong: Grandparents may come more often, and they will take me to the zoo beside the sea.

Mother: Yes, that's one thing. But there is something more important. Come and sit here. I'll tell you a story. In the 1830s — that's a very long time ago — British merchants began to smuggle opium into China from India.

Dongdong: What does "smuggle opium" mean?

Mother: It means selling opium to our Chinese without the permission of the Chinese government. Opium is a kind of poison to human beings. China had banned the opium trade several years before that.

Dongdong: I know now. I won't take opium, Mom.

Mother: Good boy. But the British went on poisoning our Chinese. Later, a national hero named Lin Zexu confiscated a lot of opium and burnt it in Canton. The British used this as a pretext and launched a war of aggression against China. (*There is a puzzled expression in Dongdong's face.*) Just like the Japanese invaded our China decades ago. (*Dongdong nods.*) By *the Treaty of Nanking* in 1842, China ceded Hong Kong to Britain. It's not until now that Hong Kong is going to return. Do you understand now?

Dongdong: Yes, I'll welcome the return of Hong Kong just like welcoming Mom home after work.

Mother: When you go to kindergarten tomorrow morning, you may test other boys and girls to see if they already know the story. If not, you may tell them the story, right?

Dongdong: Yes, that's a good idea.

Mother: Now, let's watch TV.

Part Three Compound Dictation

Farewell to Hong Kong

1) administration
2) coastal
3) courage
4) dramatic
5) societies
6) framework
7) resourceful
8) More than three and a half million Hong Kong residents are British nationals
9) The shared legacy of family and of friendship, trade and investment, culture and history runs strong and deep
10) We are confident that the ties between us will not only endure but will continue to develop

Tapescript

Governor, Prime Minister, ladies and gentlemen, I've been asked by Her Majesty the Queen to read the following message.

Five hours from now the Union flag will be lowered and the flag of China will fly over Hong Kong. More than a century and a half of British administration will come to an end. During that time Hong Kong has grown from a small coastal settlement into one of the leading cities and one of the greatest trading economies in the world. There have been times of sacrifice, suffering and courage. As Hong Kong has risen from the ashes of war, a most dramatic transformation has taken place; millions of destitute immigrants have been absorbed and Hong Kong has created one of the most successful societies on earth. Britain is both proud and privileged to be involved with this success story. Proud of the British values and institutions that have been the framework for Hong Kong's success. Proud of the rights and freedoms which Hong Kong people enjoy. Privileged to be associated with the prodigiously talented and resourceful people of Hong Kong who have built upon that foundation. The British flag will be lowered and British administrative responsibility will end. But Britain is not saying good-bye to Hong Kong. More than three and a half million Hong Kong residents are British nationals. Thousands of young Hong Kong men and women study in Britain every year. We share language and the English Common Law. And thousands of Britons too, have made their homes in Hong Kong. The shared legacy of family and of friendship, trade and investment, culture and history runs strong and deep. Britain is part of Hong Kong's history and Hong Kong is part of Britain's history. We are also part of each other's future. We are confident that the ties between us will not only endure but will continue to develop. The eyes of the world are on Hong Kong today. I wish you all a successful transition and a prosperous and peaceful future.

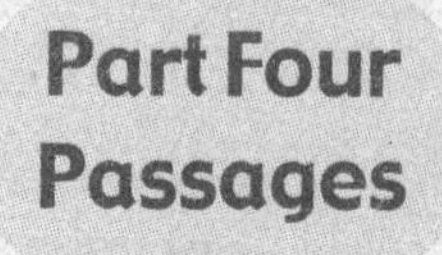

Part Four Passages

A. Blood, Toil, Sweat and Tears

1. 1) That this House welcomes the formation of a government representing the united and inflexible resolve of the nation to prosecute the war with Germany to a victorious conclusion.
   2) I have nothing to offer but blood, toil, tears and sweat.
   3) No survival for the British Empire, no survival for all that the British Empire has stood for, no survival for the urge, the impulse of the ages, that mankind shall move forward toward his goal.
2. 1) C 2) D 3) B 4) C 5) A

Tapescript

I now invite the House by a resolution to record its approval of the steps taken and declare its confidence in the new government. The resolution:

"That this House welcomes the formation of a government representing the united and inflexible resolve of the nation to prosecute the war with Germany to a victorious conclusion."

To form an administration of this scale and complexity is a serious undertaking in itself. But we are in the preliminary phase of one of the greatest battles in history. We are in action at many other points — in Norway and in Holland — and we have to be prepared in the Mediterranean. The air battle is continuing, and many preparations have to be made here at home.

I say to the House as I said to Ministers who have joined this government, I have nothing to offer but blood, toil, tears and sweat. We have before us an ordeal of the most grievous kind. We have before us many, many months of struggle and suffering.

You ask, what is our policy? I say it is to wage war by land, sea and air. War with all our might and with all the strength God has given us, and to wage war against a monstrous tyranny never surpassed in the dark and lamentable catalogue of human crime. That is our policy.

You ask, what is our aim? I can answer in one word. It is victory. Victory at all costs — victory in spite of all terrors — victory, however long and hard the road may be, for without victory there is no survival.

Let that be realized. No survival for the British Empire, no survival for all that the British Empire has stood for, no survival for the urge, the impulse of the ages, that mankind shall move forward toward his goal.

I take up my task in buoyancy and hope. I feel sure that our cause will not be suffered to fail among men.

I feel entitled at this juncture, at this time, to claim the aid of all and to say, "Come then, let us go forward together with our united strength."

Sentence dictation:

1) That this House welcomes the formation of a government representing the united and inflexible resolve of the nation to prosecute the war with Germany to a victorious conclusion.
2) I have nothing to offer but blood, toil, tears and sweat.
3) No survival for the British Empire, no survival for all that the British Empire has stood for, no survival for the urge, the impulse of the ages, that mankind shall move forward toward his goal.

B. Commencement Address at Harvard University

1. 1) D 2) A 3) B 4) C 5) C

Tapescript

President Rudenstine, fellow graduates, friends of Harvard,

It is a great honor and pleasure to be invited today to share this happy occasion, not only with the members of the graduating class of 1998, but also with the families and friends who have no doubt supported you along the way with their kind words of advice and encouragement. I do remember sitting where so many of you sat this morning when I was a part of the class of 1968. I still remember how uncertain and insecure I felt but how proud my father was on the day. Your families and your professors are rightfully proud of your achievements and they are delighted to see you graduate with futures so bright with promise.

I too am proud. I am proud to see so many capable young men and women about to embark on a future career where they can put their years of learning and preparation to good use. Having passed through the rigors of a formal education, you are now ready to assume new responsibilities and tasks, become answerable only to yourselves with regard to your performance, your humanity and your soundness of judgment, in a world full of possibilities.

But I would ask you to remember that it is not a world full of possibilities for all. Each of you has been the beneficiary of a rare privilege. You have received an exceptional education at an exceptional place when there are many, in both your country and mine, and in many, many other parts of our world, who are just as innately talented and just as ambitious as you are but will never have such an opportunity. I say this not to make you feel guilty. You should be proud of what you have achieved. But I do ask that you use your education to pursue only the worthiest of goals; goals that contribute to the betterment of the lives of others; and goals that give you personal satisfaction because of their contribution to the society we live in.

It's only to say but I wish you much happiness and success in the years ahead. May your memories of Harvard, as mine are, and the friends you have made here, be with you always. Congratulations to the new graduates and I am very honored to be linked with the undergraduates of the class of 1998, and be rejuvenated by joining the class of 1998. Thank you very much!

Unit Nine Economic Development

Part One Short Conversations

1. C 2. B 3. A 4. A 5. A 6. A 7. D 8. D
9. C 10. A 11. D 12. C 13. D 14. B 15. C

Tapescript

1. ***M***: How many students took the exam last Friday?
   W: Well, fifty had registered, but only half of them showed up.
   Q: How many students were absent from the test?
2. ***M***: Could you please tell me if Flight 309 will be arriving on time?
   W: Yes, Sir. It should be arriving in about 15 minutes.
   Q: Where did the conversation most probably take place?
3. ***W***: I want to buy some books on art, but they are so expensive.
   M: The library has many books on art.
   Q: What does the man imply?
4. ***M***: How could John speak Spanish so fluently?
   W: Oh, he spent a year in Spain and came back speaking Spanish as he does.
   Q: What can be said of John?
5. ***M***: Did you go shopping?
   W: Yes, but all I got was a sore foot.
   Q: What does the woman mean?
6. ***W***: How do I look in my new dress?
   M: It fits you like a glove and matches your eyes perfectly.
   Q: What does the man think of the woman's new dress?
7. ***W***: Peter can't help finding fault with everything.
   M: That's why Ruth becomes so angry at him and decides to break up their engagement.
   Q: What do we learn from the conversation?
8. ***M***: How did you get the theater tickets?
   W: One of the director's friends gave them to me, but they weren't free, I paid for

them.

Q: How did the woman get the tickets?

9. *W*: If you can help me paint the bookshelf and the table this morning, we can go to the beach this afternoon.

   M: I'm not very good at painting, but if you like I'll wash the car instead.

   Q: What is the man going to do this morning?

10. *M*: I thought Amy majored in mathematics in college, but now she has just found a job as an engineer in a building company.

    W: That's true. After studying mathematics for three years, she changed her major to architecture.

    Q: What is true of Amy?

11. *M*: Didn't you say you'd drive me to the airport?

    W: Right. We'll leave immediately after the news.

    Q: What are these people going to do?

12. *M*: The children want something for a snack.

    W: Don't give them anything. They're going to have dinner soon.

    Q: What is the man going to give the children?

13. *M*: I'd better get going if I want to get home before dark.

    W: Give my best to Ann and the kids.

    Q: What do we learn from this conversation?

14. *M*: I'd like to cash this check.

    W: You can do that only if you have an account with us. Do you have one?

    Q: What does the man want?

15. *M*: Why don't we go to Las Vegas this summer?

    W: We can't go through the Death Valley in our old car. We'll have to save some money and go by plane.

    Q: What are they going to do this summer?

Part Two Dialogue

Scientific Breakthroughs in the 21st Century

1. 1) B 2) C 3) D 4) D
2. 1) an astonishing speed

2) big scientific breakthroughs
3) develop theories; evolution of the universe
4) life expectancy

Tapescript

A: It's the 21st century now, and everything is developing at an astonishing speed, especially the technology.
B: Yes, I've learned from the newspaper that it is predicted that there will be some big scientific breakthroughs in this century.
A: What are they?
B: First, we'll know where we came from. In other words, why is there something instead of nothing. Scientists will develop theories presenting detailed picture of the evolution of the universe from the time it was a fraction of a second old to the present.
A: Then we will know how and why the universe exists.
B: Yes. As to human beings, we'll crack the genetic code and conquer cancer.
A: Then cancer will no longer be a killer of human beings. But how?
B: Using manufactured " therapeutic" viruses, doctors will be able to replace cancer using DNA with healthy genes, probably by a pill or injection.
A: That will definitely lead to longer life expectancy of human beings, right?
B: Yes. There will be another breakthrough in this century. Development in genetic medicine may let us control and even reverse the aging process. Maybe we can live 120 years!
A: If all you said turns true, we are so lucky to live in this century.

Part Three Compound Dictation

The Japanese Economy

1) predicting
2) range
3) sharply
4) indications
5) average
6) estimated
7) expansion

8) After last year's extraordinary growth of Japanese exports, there has been some slowdown in export growth

9) This year's wage increases were bigger than last year's and, on top of that, workers have received a good summer bonus

10) Semiconductors have taken the lead in Japan's electronics boom

Tapescript

Japan's economic expansion is showing solid strength and staying power. We are predicting that the annual growth rate of real GNP for both this year and the next will be in the four-to-five-percent range. In particular, for this year as a whole, it will wind up at the high end of that range.

In the first quarter, real GNP growth dropped off sharply to an annual rate of only four-tenths of one percent. But that is no cause for alarm; Japan's growth rate swings very widely from one quarter to the next, and there are already many indications that it has swung back up in the second quarter.

In the fourth quarter of last year, real growth shot up at an annual 9.6%. So the average for the new quarters, fourth quarter and first, is 5%. But in any case, in the second quarter, which just ended, industrial output leaped back up at an estimated rate of 11.8% — after a first-quarter decline of 2.7%. So you see, the expansion remains strong and you can expect it to stay on track.

After last year's extraordinary growth of Japanese exports, there has been some slowdown in export growth. That was to be expected. But even at this slower pace, export growth will remain a pillar of the economic expansion.

But now the expansion is also drawing strength from a recovery in domestic demand and from a continuing vigor in capital spending. This year's wage increases were bigger than last year's and, on top of that, workers have received a good summer bonus. With inflation running below 2%, the result has been a gradual recovery in consumer sales and in spending on travel and entertaining.

But perhaps a more positive factor has been resilient strength in capital spending. Its tempo has slowed a bit. The semiconductor industry, for instance, has trimmed its capital spending plans because demand for its products has slowed. Semiconductors have taken the lead in Japan's electronics boom. Still, across the economy, corporate profits are way up , and we expect that this year, in real terms, capital spending will rise 7% – 8%.

Part Four Passages

A. E-money

1. 1) C   2) D   3) C   4) D
2. 1) F   2) F   3) T   4) T   5) T

Tapescript

Just imagine: no coins in your pants, no bills in your wallet. To buy a soda you simply insert something called value card into the vending machine. A text display above the slot where you once dropped quarters tells you how much is being deducted and the remaining value on the card. You pull out the same card to board a bus, do your laundry, or buy a newspaper. You add value to the card by inserting it in an Automatic Teller Machine. Once e-money is accepted as universally as dollars, don't be surprised if a man on the street steps up to you and says, " Excuse me, can you spare a little stored value?"

What makes a smart card like cash is that it is a debit card rather than a credit card: it already has value.

Why cards instead of cash or check? Convenience, security, and cost. Money costs money. Handling it, accounting for it, protecting and tracking it is expensive — whether the money is in the form of cash, checks, or credit cards — to the tune of $ 60 billion a year by one reckoning. Money wears out. Checks must be handled and stored. Credit cards must be manufactured and billed. The amounts of transactions must be verified by phone. Today's bill are problematic for vending machines. Modern vending machines accept dollar bills, but users still face the frustration of their money being rejected because of folded corners and wrinkled edges.

One of the great benefits of smart cards is that the card's value can be verified and changed without going through the kind of credit card dial-up system. Transactions can be speeded up, and lines shortened.

Smart cards are moving us toward a cashless society. The money of the future is likely to be smarter, smaller, and more versatile than today's currency.

B. The US Economy

1. 1) A 2) C 3) B 4) B
2. 1) T 2) T 3) T 4) F

Tapescript

Generally, economists have fallen into two camps in analyzing what is going on in the economy right now. One group has viewed the strength of the service sector, the construction industry, and the auto industry as being the engine of growth, heading to a rebound in the manufacturing sector. We are obviously in that camp.

Others have forecast that the malaise in the manufacturing industries would spread throughout the economy, damping the growth in consumer income and spending and reducing the need for businesses to invest in capital goods. Real GNP would remain sluggish, and some feel that we could get a recession.

Some maintain that the consumers are overextended in terms of credit. This is a typical reaction — at this stage of the business cycle, analysts always point to a large gap between consumer income growth and consumer credit growth. But debt always rises faster than income during recession years.

If we go back and look at the last 20 years and remove the zigs and zags produced by business cycles, we find that both consumer credit as well as consumer income have generally risen 9% – 10% per year on average, so this is fairly normal. The continuing rise in consumer real income and wealth has made a larger proportion of families creditworthy. And we feel this has increased their willingness to borrow.

One final bone of contention between forecasters is how they view business capital spending. Some analysts perceive that the weakness in the economy and in corporate profits will damp the willingness to spend. Now, to be sure, real capital outlays will not match that 15% – 16% real rate of increase they had last year but they are not going to grind to a halt, either. We have had the strongest investment recovery on record, and most of this investment was going to plant modernization and productivity enhancing , not to build new capacity. So it is our view that the competitive need to boost labor productivity and lower break-even points in a very competitive global market will result in second-half capital outlays, particularly for office equipment, that will surprise the pessimists.

Unit Ten Chinese Culture

Part One Short Conversations

1. A 2. A 3. D 4. D 5. D 6. D 7. A 8. B
9. C 10. B 11. A 12. B 13. A 14. D 15. B

Tapescript

1. *M*: The telegram just came from Mary. She will arrive at 2 o'clock.
   W: Oh, good. She can rest a few hours before the concert.
   Q: What can Mary do after she arrives?
2. *M*: I'd like to check in, please.
   W: May I have your tickets, please? Thank you. Here's your boarding pass, sir. Please go to the Departure Lounge. Your flight will be called in 15 minutes.
   Q: Where does the conversation most probably take place?
3. *M*: Have Tom's parents left for Los Angeles yet?
   W: I think so. I called their house last night, but there was no answer. They probably left on Monday.
   Q: What did the man learn from the woman?
4. *M*: These yellow gloves and those red ones seem about the same as far as quality is concerned. Is there any difference in price?
   W: The yellow ones are $3.40 a pair, but the red ones are on sale today for $3.15. They were $3.60 a pair last week.
   Q: How much will the man pay if he buys two pairs of red gloves?
5. *W*: I was sorry to hear about your accident.
   M: Well, it could have been worse. If it had happened a little further along the road, my car would have landed in the river instead of that grassy field.
   Q: What happened to the man's car?
6. *M*: Could you drive a car when you were 16 years old?
   W: No, and I still can't drive a car. I go everywhere by bus.
   Q: What do we learn about the woman?
7. *W*: Oh, no. It's a quarter to five already and I'll miss my 5 o'clock train.

***M*:** Don't worry. That clock is half an hour fast. You have enough time to catch it.

***Q*:** When does this conversation take place?

8. ***M*:** Are you going to the dance party tonight?

***W*:** No. I have to type a history paper which is due tomorrow morning.

***Q*:** What will the woman do tonight?

9. ***M*:** Operator, I'd like to make a call to Rome, please. How much will it cost?

***W*:** $10 for the first three minutes and 2 for each additional minute.

***Q*:** How much will a ten-minute call cost?

10. ***W*:** Are you still working in the hospital?

***M*:** Not since July. My brother and I went into business together as soon as he graduated from college.

***Q*:** What can we learn about the man from this conversation?

11. ***W*:** I never thought I'd see your name on a book cover.

***M*:** To tell you the truth, neither did I. I didn't even get good grades in English.

***Q*:** What is the man's profession?

12. ***M*:** Aren't you going to apologize for breaking that window?

***W*:** Why should I? I didn't throw the ball.

***Q*:** How does the woman feel about the situation?

13. ***W*:** I just got my first issue of that new magazine.

***M*:** Let me see it when you're through. Maybe I'll subscribe, too.

***Q*:** What is the man going to do?

14. ***W*:** This package was returned to me.

***M*:** That's because you didn't put enough postage on it.

***Q*:** What did the man tell the woman about the package?

15. ***M*:** Want to come to the beach with me if it doesn't rain?

***W*:** No, I don't think so. It's very hot out and I burn easily.

***Q*:** Why won't the woman go to the beach?

Part Two Dialogue

China Culture Week

1. 1) B 2) C 3) A 4) D 5) D

2. 1) a) To help the British people and people from other parts of the world learn about the

past and the present of China.

b) To promote the exchanges between China and the UK and the understanding of the two cultures./ To narrow the distance between the East and the West.

2) Subjects that represent the essence of Chinese culture, both ancient and modern.

3) a) exhibitions

b) performances

4) Beijing Opera originated from Beijing some 200 years ago.

5) a) The ancient clothes of different dynasties from Qin to Han.

b) The costumes of China's ethnic groups.

c) Modern garments and accessories.

3. Suggested answer:

1) exhibition of ink painting

2) Chinese classic book fair

3) exhibition of silk products

Tapescript

Q: China has held many cultural exchange activities in Europe and many other parts of the world. The coming China Culture Week is the largest cultural exhibition of its kind. May I know the purpose of staging such an exhibition?

A: We have entered the new millennium. We hope that the exhibition will help the British people and people from other parts of the world learn about the past and the present of China. Meanwhile, the Culture Week is expected to promote the exchanges between China and the UK and the understanding of the two cultures, and narrow the distance between the East and the West.

Q: What will be displayed within the seven days?

A: We have selected some subjects that represent the essence of Chinese culture, both ancient and modern. The activities are of two major types: exhibitions and performances.

Q: Could you tell me more about the exhibition?

A: Well, it includes the achievements of China's education, culture, architecture, science and technology. We'll show you the new outlook of the capital city of Beijing and Shanghai as well as the best works of Chinese pottery, costumes of Beijing Opera, Chinese chimes and cultural relics unearthed in China.

Q: What about the Beijing Opera costumes to be displayed?

A: Beijing Opera originated from Beijing some 200 years ago during the Qing Dynasty. It's a performing art that embraces opera performance, singing, music, dancing and martial arts. The costume exposition will present 200 years of development of the "Oriental Opera" and the performing costume dating back to the late Qing Dynasty. The costume design adopted exaggeration and symbolic means and bright colors. The materials are unique, so are the tailoring skills. Another exhibition will display a total of 600 sets of clothes, including the ancient clothes of different dynasties from Qin to Han, the costumes of China's ethnic groups, and modern garments and accessories. Famous models from the mainland will participate to present the achievements of the Chinese garment industry and Chinese designers.

Q: Thank you very much for the introduction. I wish the coming China Culture Week a complete success.

A: Thanks, and expect to see you again at the exhibition.

Part Three Compound Dictation

Traditional Celebration of the Chinese New Year

1) elaborate
2) congratulate
3) corresponding
4) reunions
5) stresses
6) ties
7) occasions
8) Typical preparations for the Chinese New Year in old China start well in advance of the New Year's Day
9) Every corner of the house must be swept and cleaned in preparation for the New Year
10) In addition, symbolic flowers and fruits are used to decorate the house, and colorful new year pictures called NIAN HUA are placed on the walls

Tapescript

Of all the traditional Chinese festivals, the Chinese New Year is perhaps the most elaborate, colorful, and important. This is a time for the Chinese to congratulate each other and themselves on having passed through another year, a time to finish out the old, and to welcome in the New Year.

The Chinese New Year is celebrated on the first day of the First Moon of the lunar calendar. The corresponding date in the solar calendar varies from as early as January 21st to as late as February 19th. Chinese New Year, as the Western New Year, signified turning over a new leaf. Socially, it is a time for family reunions, and for visiting friends and relatives. This holiday, more than any other Chinese holiday, stresses the importance of family ties. The Chinese New Year's Eve dinner gathering is among the most important family occasions of the year.

Typical preparations for the Chinese New Year in old China start well in advance of the New Year's Day. The 20th of the Twelfth Moon is set aside for the annual housecleaning, or the "sweeping of the grounds". Every corner of the house must be swept and cleaned in preparation for the New Year. Spring Couplets, written in black ink on large vertical scrolls of red paper, are put on the walls or on the sides of the gateways. These couplets, short poems written in Classical Chinese, are expressions of good wishes for the family in the coming year. In addition, symbolic flowers and fruits are used to decorate the house, and colorful new year pictures called NIAN HUA are placed on the walls.

Part Four Passages

A. Lu Xun

1. 3), 4), 6), 9), 10)

2.

Time	Major Events in Lu Xun's Life
1902	He went to Japan to study medicine.
1906	He abruptly terminated his medical studies to devote himself to literary endeavors.
1909	He returned to China.
1918	He wrote Diary of a Madman.
in the 1920s	He taught Chinese literature at universities in Beijing and other cities.
toward the end of his life	He founded the League of Left-Wing Writers.

Tapescript

Lu Xun is China's foremost modern writer and intellectual, whose works have exerted a profound impact on modern Chinese literature and society. A household name throughout China, Lu Xun is generally acknowledged as a leader of the May Fourth Movement, a 1919 revolution that sought to modernize Chinese social and intellectual life.

Born in Shaoxing, a city in Eastern China, he received a traditional education with family tutors before entering school in Nanjing. In 1902 he went to Japan to study medicine, but in 1906 he abruptly terminated his medical studies to devote himself to literary endeavors. He believed that only through literature could he possibly reform Chinese society and change the collective soul of his people. After returning to China in 1909 and emerging from a period of mental depression, Lu Xun achieved literary renown in 1918 with the short story *Kuangren Riji* (*Diary of a Madman*). The story appeared in *The New Youth*, a journal that initiated the May Fourth or New Culture Movement. Because it was written in the contemporary vernacular and offered a devastating critique of traditional Chinese culture, it has been hailed as China's first modern story. Two collections of short stories followed in the 1920s, during which time Lu Xun taught Chinese literature at universities in Beijing and other cities.

Throughout his creative life Lu Xun was deeply tormented by a conflict between his inner pessimism and his public stance in favor of building a new Chinese nation and society. These struggles carried over into his creative writings, in which he experimented with a variety of techniques and genres. Toward the end of his life, he settled in the cosmopolitan city of Shanghai, turned to Communism, and founded the League of Left-Wing Writers.

In addition to his short stories, Lu Xun also produced 16 volumes of essays; a collection of personal reminiscences, prose poetry, and historical tales; about 60 poems in the classical style; half a dozen volumes of scholarly research, primarily on Chinese fiction; and translations of numerous works of Russian, Eastern European, and Japanese literature.

B. "What's This" or "This Is What"?

1. 1) C　2) D　3) A　4) A　5) B
2. 1) give perfect pronunciation
   2) the romantic type
   3) prefer the "old spouse" formula

4) he was introducing his "boss" instead of his "old spouse"

5) two contradictory views

6) no gender, no case, no number

7) no tense, no voice and no mood

8) no agreement of subject and verb

9) any classification of words

10) the simplest language in the world

3. 2) a) Pay special attention to the four tones in Chinese.

b) Practice as much as possible.

c) Learn some Chinese customs and culture.

Tapescript

I have a friend who rather prides himself on his talent for learning foreign languages. He said that when he first came to China he learned to give perfect pronunciation of all the impossible Chinese sounds within a matter of weeks. Then, one day he introduced his wife to some Chinese friends. He said "this is my wife" in Chinese, but, as he was told afterwards, what he actually succeeded in saying was "this is my piece of chess". He was also told that Chinese seldom introduced their wives by saying, "This is my wife," they say, "This is my old spouse" or, "This is my sweetheart", instead. Now this friend of mine is not the romantic type, so he decided he would prefer the "old spouse" formula. But when the time came for him to try that out, he found to his disappointment again that people thought he was introducing his "boss" instead of his "old spouse". It's a matter of tone, they say. This mystery of tone in Chinese language — is it really so incomprehensible to us foreigners?

Learning to speak Chinese is difficult enough for us Westerners. But learning to write Chinese is even more frustrating. There is a joke about an Englishman who remarks about the Chinese language: "I don't want to learn a language which tolerates sentences like 'This is what?'" Now I understand the Chinese language and the English language have one feature in common in that they both depend very much on word order.

Whenever I ask about the grammar of the Chinese language, I find people give me very different answers. These answers represent two contradictory views. One view is that Chinese is a language without grammar. Because the Chinese nouns and pronouns have no gender, no case, no number and the Chinese verbs have no tense, no voice and no mood. There is no agreement of subject and verb, no strict pattern of a grammatical sentence, and not even any classification of words. In fact, there is not anything. They make Chinese sound like the simplest language in the world. The other view believes Chinese is the most complicated language in the world. Which of these views is nearer the truth?

Unit Eleven Philosophy of Life

Part One Short Conversations

1. B 2. C 3. A 4. A 5. D 6. C 7. A 8. A
9. D 10. A 11. C 12. A 13. A 14. A 15. C

Tapescript

1. *W*: What did you do after the literature class?
   M: I went to the library to return some books, and then did some shopping.
   Q: What did the man do first?
2. *W*: Mike, do you think it is possible for you to check my mailbox while I'm gone?
   M: Sure, Nancy, I will take care of that.
   Q: What does the woman want the man to do?
3. *M*: I'd like to have some chocolate cakes and a glass of orange juice to follow the main course. Would you want the same?
   W: No, thanks. I'm on a diet.
   Q: What does the woman mean?
4. *W*: I can't imagine why Jane hasn't arrived. She was due before now.
   M: It's rush hour, dear.
   Q: What does the man imply?
5. *M*: Liz took a taxi to her office today.
   W: Yes. Her friend Ted usually drives her to the office but now he is out of town on business.
   Q: What do we learn from the conversation?
6. *M*: Helen doesn't take a part-time job this semester.
   W: No. Her grades enabled her to earn a scholarship.
   Q: What is implied about Helen?
7. *W*: I've got to go to New York this afternoon, but I'm too tired to drive and the bus is so uncomfortable.
   M: No problem. I'll drop you off at the train station on my way to work.
   Q: How is the man getting to work?

8. *W*: What time is it by your watch?

M: 8:50. I set my watch by the radio this morning.

W: I guess mine is fast. I have 8:55.

Q: What can you learn about the woman's watch?

9. *W*: I was hoping we both will be in the psychology class.

M: Me too, Amy. But by the time I got to the registration the class was closed.

Q: What does the man mean?

10. *W*: I've been having trouble with my term paper. Would it be convenient to see you today?

M: I'm afraid not, Jenny. But tomorrow my office hour lasts from 10:00 to noon.

Q: Who is the man?

11. *W*: This house costs $68,500. That's a lot of money.

M: It's worth every penny of it.

Q: What did the man mean?

12. *M*: I'm told that you have a baby. Is it he or she?

W: A pretty girl. How do you know that?

Q: Which is mentioned in the dialogue?

13. *W*: Do you want some more fruit?

M: No, thank you. I'm on a diet.

Q: Which of the following is true?

14. *W*: OK. Don't move and say cheese.

M: Wait a moment, please. I forgot to put on my hat.

Q: Which of the following is true?

15. *W*: I have no brain for dancing. I can't improve it at all.

M: Good heavens! There is no room for improvement.

Q: Which of the following can describe the woman's dancing?

Part Two
Dialogue

Most Important Thing Is to Be Happy

1. 1), 4)

2.

	Mrs. Lee's View	Carl's View
Job and Money	find a better job and make more money	settle down and put some roots into the ground
Love and Family	If you have a little bit of love for someone, it's OK to marry.	wait for the right moment prefer natural love be happy

Tapescript

L: *Mrs. Lee* ***C***: *Carl*

L: My son is 32 years old. Ah ... Carl, I don't understand what goes on in his young head sometimes.

C: Is he acting strange, Mrs. Lee?

L: He wants to quit his job and find another. He told me he wants to find a better job and to make more money.

C: Sounds normal to me. It's pretty much what I want to do. Even my friends are like this.

L: What about settling down and starting a family? Doesn't anyone want to get married anymore, you know, put some roots into the ground?

C: It's different now. The world is becoming a very lively place. My friends don't feel the same pressure to marry. We all want to wait for the right moment.

L: Where do you find the right moment?

C: Let the universe find us instead of forcing love. We prefer natural love.

L: You know, when I was young our parents taught us that if you have a little bit of love for someone it's OK to marry.

C: How does that work? How could you spend your whole life with someone that you don't love?

L: As each day grows, so will your love.

C: And if it doesn't?

L: We just do the best we can. Now, I'm hoping that my children can do better than my husband and I did. It is difficult to watch my son doing what he is doing.

C: Most important thing is to be happy. Love will find us later. That is what we say.

Part Three Compound Dictation

Bias for Beauty

1) indication
2) understandable
3) distinct
4) applicants
5) irrational
6) competence
7) virtue
8) It is not surprising that physical attractiveness is of overwhelming importance to us
9) But although we resemble our ancestors and other cultures in our concern about appearance, there is a difference in degree of concern
10) They often don't trust praise of their work or talents, believing positive evaluations to be influenced by their appearance

Tapescript

We are all more obsessed with our appearance than we like to admit. But this is not an indication of "vanity". Vanity means conceit, excessive pride in one's appearance. Concern about appearance is quite normal and understandable. Attractive people have distinct advantages in our society. Attractive children are more popular, both with classmates and teachers. Attractive applicants have a better chance of getting jobs, and of receiving higher salaries.

We also believe in the "what is beautiful is good" stereotype — an irrational but deep-seated belief that physically attractive people possess other desirable characteristics such as intelligence, competence, social skills, confidence — even moral virtue. The good fairy is always beautiful; the wicked stepmother is always ugly.

It is not surprising that physical attractiveness is of overwhelming importance to us.

Concern with appearance is not just a phenomenon of Modern Western Culture. Every period of history has had its own standards of what is and is not beautiful, and every contemporary society has its own distinctive concept of the ideal physical attributes. Now we try to diet and exercise ourselves into the fashionable shape — often with even more serious consequences. But although we resemble our ancestors and other cultures in our concern about appearance, there is a difference in degree of concern. Advances in technology and in particular the rise of the mass media has caused normal concerns about how we look to become obsessions.

Even very attractive people may not be looking in the mirror out of "vanity", but out of insecurity. We forget that there are disadvantages to being attractive: attractive people are under much greater pressure to maintain their appearance. Also, studies show that attractive people don't benefit from the "bias for beauty" in terms of self-esteem. They often don't trust praise of their work or talents, believing positive evaluations to be influenced by their appearance.

Part Four Passages

A. Laziness

1. 1) B 2) C 3) D 4) B 5) A
2. 1) Laziness is a sin./ Laziness is immoral, that it is wasteful./Lazy people will never amount to anything in life.
   2) They may be so distrustful of their fellow workers that they are unable to join in any group task for fear of ridicule or fear of having their ideas stolen.
   3) Some great scientific discoveries occurred by chance or while someone was "goofing off".
   4) For those who overwork themselves (such as overworked student or executive, the athlete who is trying too hard or the doctor who's simply working himself overtime too many evenings at the clinic).

Tapescript

Laziness is a sin, everyone knows that. We have probably had all lectures pointing out that laziness is immoral, that it is wasteful, and that lazy people will never amount to anything in life. But laziness can be more harmful than that, and it is often caused by more complex reasons than simple wish to avoid work. Some people who appear to be lazy are suffering from much more serious problems. They may be so distrustful of their fellow workers that they are unable to join in any group task for fear of ridicule or fear of having their ideas stolen. These people who seem lazy may be paralyzed by a fear of failure.

Nevertheless, laziness can actually be helpful. Some people may look lazy when they are really thinking, planning, contemplating, researching. We should all remember that some great scientific discoveries occurred by chance or while someone was "goofing off". Newton wasn't working in the orchard when the apple hit him and he devised the theory of gravity. All of us would like to have someone "lazy" build the car or stove we buy, particularly if that "laziness" were caused by the worker's taking time to check each step of his work and to do his job right. And sometimes being "lazy"—that is, taking time off for a rest — is good for the overworked student or executive. Taking a rest can be particularly helpful to the athlete who is trying too hard or the doctor who's simply working himself overtime too many evenings at the clinic. So be careful when you're tempted to call someone lazy. That person may be thinking, or planning his or her next book.

B. Paradox of Our Times

1. 1) D 2) B 3) A 4) G 5) C 6) J 7) E 8) I 9) F 10) H
2. 1) inconceivable to our ancestors; more chances and challenges than ever
   2) bigger houses and smaller families; more experts, but more problems
   3) get angry too quickly; pray too seldom
   4) multiplied our possessions; added years to life
   5) crossing the street to meet the new neighbor; not inner space; not our prejudice; accomplish less
   6) hold more information; short on quality
3. 1) 这是一个快餐食品和消化迟缓相伴的时代，一个体格高大和性格狭隘并存的时代，一个追名逐利和人情冷漠相生的时代。
   2) 我们获得了一张又一张学位证书，却愈加频繁地陷入对常识的茫然中；我们广泛地涉猎各类知识，却越来越缺乏对于外界事物的准确判断；专家越来越多，问题日渐增加；药物越吃越多，健康却每况愈下。
   3) 我们掌握了谋生手段，却不懂得生活真谛；我们让年华付诸流水，却不曾将生命倾注其中。
   4) 我们能够往返于地球与月球之间，却不善于穿过马路向新邻居问好。
   5) 我们生产更多的电脑用于存储更多的信息和制造更多的拷贝，而相互间的交流与沟通却越来越少。

Tapescript

People living at the start of the third millennium enjoy a world that would have been inconceivable to our ancestors. Human beings are faced with more chances and challenges than ever. These are the times of fast foods and slow digestion; tall men and short character; steep profits and shallow relationships. More leisure and less fun; more kinds of food, but less nutrition; two incomes, but more divorce; fancier houses, but broken homes.

We have bigger houses and smaller families; more conveniences, but less time; we have more degrees, but less common sense; more knowledge, but less judgment; more experts, but more problems; more medicine, but less wellness.

We spend too recklessly, laugh too little, drive too fast, get angry too quickly, stay up too late, get up too tired, read too little, watch TV too often, and pray too seldom.

We have multiplied our possessions, but reduced our values. We talk too much, love too little and lie too often. We've learned how to make a living, but not a life; we've added years to life, not life to years.

We have taller buildings, but shorter tempers; wider freeways, but narrower viewpoints. We spend more, but have less; we buy more, but enjoy it less.

We've been all the way to the moon and back, but have trouble crossing the street to meet the new neighbor. We've conquered outer space, but not inner space. We've split the atom, but not our prejudice; we write more, but learn less; plan more, but accomplish less.

We've learned to rush, but not to wait; we have higher incomes, but lower morals. We build more computers to hold more information, to produce more copies, but have less communication. We are long on quantity, but short on quality.

Unit Twelve Law

Part One Short Conversations

1. B 2. A 3. B 4. C 5. D 6. D 7. A 8. B
9. B 10. C 11. A 12. B 13. A 14. B 15. C

Tapescript

1. ***W*:** Tomorrow I'll bring you some books. Is there anything special you'd like to eat?
   ***M*:** No. I don't feel like eating or reading either, but would you bring me a small tube of toothpaste, please?
   ***Q*:** Where are the two speakers?
2. ***M*:** Mark is very nice, but his sister is not very polite.
   ***W*:** I know, and she is much too talkative.
   ***Q*:** What do they think of Mark's sister?
3. ***W*:** Did Mary enjoy her trip on the ocean liner?
   ***M*:** No. She stayed in her cabin and vomited terribly while the ship was at sea.
   ***Q*:** What do we know about Mary?
4. ***W*:** What should I do after I put the coins in?
   ***M*:** Listen for the dialing tone, Sue, and then dial the number you want.
   ***Q*:** What is Sue learning to use?
5. ***W*:** Where did you celebrate your birthday last year?
   ***M*:** Let me see. A year ago today, I was a passenger on an Air Greece plane. I had just left my sister's home in Athens and was on my way to school in New York.
   ***Q*:** Where was the man a year ago today?
6. ***W*:** What do you want from the Woolworth's, Mike?
   ***M*:** Oh, I just need some toothpaste and a couple of other things.
   ***Q*:** Where is the woman going?
7. ***M*:** In our science classes we use kilos, but we use pounds and ounces in everyday life.

W: Your country also uses inches, feet and yards, doesn't it?

Q: What are they discussing?

8. *M*: I wonder if I could borrow your calculator, please?

   W: You certainly could if I had one, but I gave my old one to my sister when she entered high school, and I have not bought a new one yet.

   Q: What did the woman say about her calculator?

9. *W*: Did you buy anything at the clothing sale?

   M: Yes. I bought three five-dollar ties for just twelve dollars.

   Q: How much did the man pay for his three ties?

10. *W*: You promised me you wouldn't buy any more. Maybe you don't care about your health, but I do. You might think of our children.

    M: All right. I'll throw the pack away.

    Q: What has the man probably just bought?

11. *M*: I like it very much. How much do you charge?

    W: It's 10 dollars and 20 cents.

    M: I'll take it.

    Q: Which of the following is true?

12. *M*: I hate them. I'm sure I've got a low IQ.

    W: Oh, cheer up! We didn't do too badly. The fellow next to me wrote his name at the top of the paper and looked at it for three hours. He didn't write a word.

    Q: Which of the following is NOT true?

13. *M*: Can I help you?

    W: Yes. Can you show me the way to the railway station?

    Q: Which of the following may be true?

14. *M*: I love the girl majoring in literature.

    W: How come?

    Q: What does the woman mean?

15. *W*: Can you make a discount?

    M: Come on, you see, the quality is very good.

    Q: Which of the following is true?

Part Two Dialogue

Should Handguns Be Banned?

1.

	For	Against
Mike		√
Helen	√	

2. Mike: 1) There are nearly 40,000 people every year who are murdered with handguns and 16,000 accidents in homes every year involving handguns.
   2) We've the police to defend themselves.
   3) Violence only breeds more violence. The murder rate goes up every year.

   Helen: 1) People should have the right to defend themselves.
   2) It's a very violent country.
   3) You never know what the guns plans to do once someone breaks into your house.

Tapescript

Helen: The question of handguns always raises a lot of discussion in this country. What do you think, Mike?

Mike: Well, as far as I'm concerned, the law on this should be changed. Do you know there are nearly 40,000 people every year who are murdered with handguns? It is insane. Guns ought to be outlawed immediately.

Helen: I think people should have the right to defend themselves. I mean, there are so many crazy people out there. It's a very violent country, and there'd probably be just as many murders even if we did ban handguns.

Mike: But ... Why do people have to defend themselves? That's what we've got the police for. In my opinion, violence only breeds more violence. We give people guns, and the murder rate goes up every year.

Helen: Well, If someone tries to break into your house — and that happens all the time — you never know what the guy plans to do once he gets inside. That's when you need a gun.

Mike: Thing is there are something like 16,000 accidents in homes every year involving handguns. It's not the thieves who get killed. It's mothers, fathers, and kids. You really should check the facts, Helen. Then maybe you'd change your mind.

Part Three Compound Dictation

The Court System in the USA

1) lowest
2) violated
3) determine
4) judge
5) appeal
6) witnesses
7) attempting
8) The only issue in a Court of Appeals is whether or not correct trial procedure was followed
9) The Supreme Court Justices have the option of whether or not they wish to hear the case; four Justices must vote to hear it in order to have it brought before the Court
10) The ruling of the US Supreme Court is final, though a future Court may overturn that decision

Tapescript

Although each state is free to arrange its own court system, most states justice systems have several features in common. The lowest level court in trials where state law is alleged to have been violated is the trial court. This is the only court with the power to determine the actual facts involved in a case. If either party involved in the case feels that the trial judge made an error in one of his rulings, they can appeal, or bring the case to a Court of Appeals. Whereas trials are focused around the testimony of witnesses concerning their actions or observations, appeals feature two attorneys attempting to convince a panel of five judges that the law favors their side. The only issue in a Court of Appeals is whether or not correct trial procedure was followed.

Attorneys prepare written briefs citing historical precedents and rulings to persuade the panel of judges to rule in their favor. If unsatisfied with the court's ruling, a party can ask for a Writ of Certiorari, which is essentially an appeal to the state Supreme Court. The Supreme Court Justices have the option of whether or not they wish to hear the case; four Justices must vote to hear it in order to have it brought before the Court. Out of the approximately 5,000 cases each year appealed to the United States Supreme Court, it actually hears between 100–125 of them. The procedure at this level is similar to that at the appeals court; each attorney addresses the panel of Justices, which can interrupt at almost any time with questions. The ruling of the US Supreme Court is final, though a future Court may overturn that decision.

Part Four Passages

A. What Is A Lawyer?

1. 1) F 2) F 3) T 4) T 5) T
2. 1) Complete four years of college.
   2) Complete three years at an accredited law school.
   3) Pass a state examination, which usually lasts for two or three days. It tests knowledge in all areas of law and in professional ethics and responsibility.
   4) Pass a character and fitness review. Each applicant for a law license must be approved by a committee that investigates his or her character and background.
   5) Take an oath swearing to uphold the laws and the state and federal constitutions.
   6) Receive a license from the state supreme court.

Tapescript

A lawyer is a licensed professional who advises and represents others in legal matters.

A lawyer normally spends more time in an office than in a courtroom. The "practice of law" most often involves researching legal documents, investigating facts, writing and preparing legal documents, giving advice, and settling disputes. Laws change constantly, and new cases regularly alter the meanings of laws. For these reasons, a lawyer must put much time into knowing how the laws and the changes will affect each circumstance.

A lawyer has two main duties: to uphold the law and to protect a client's rights. To carry out these duties, a lawyer must have both knowledge of the law and good communication skills.

To understand how laws and the legal system work together, lawyers must go through special schooling. The state has enacted standards that must be met before any person will be licensed to practice law, a person must:

— complete four years of college.

— complete three years at an accredited law school.

— pass a state examination, which usually lasts for two or three days. It tests knowledge in all areas of law and in professional ethics and responsibility.

— pass a character and fitness review. Each applicant for a law license must be approved by a committee that investigates his or her character and background.

— take an oath swearing to uphold the laws and the state and federal constitutions.

— receive a license from the state supreme court.

Most lawyers concentrate on one or a few specific areas, including: business law, domestic relations, labor law, criminal law, personal injury, real estate, taxation, immigration, and intellectual property law, etc.

B. The Congress

1. 1) A 2) C 3) B 4) D

2. 1) parliamentary bodies 2) equal legislative functions and powers
   3) originate revenue bills 4) appropriation bills
   5) equal legislative powers 6) not appropriate

Tapescript

Unlike some other parliamentary bodies, both the Senate and the House of Representatives have equal legislative functions and powers with certain exceptions. For example, the Constitution provides that only the House of Representatives originate revenue bills. By tradition, the House also originates appropriation bills. As both bodies have equal legislative powers, the designation of one as the "upper" House and the other as the "lower" House is not appropriate.

The chief function of Congress is making laws. In addition, the Senate has the function of advising and consenting to treaties and to certain nominations by the President. However, under the 25th Amendment to the Constitution, both Houses confirm the President's nomination for Vice President when there is a vacancy in that office. In the matter of impeachments, the House of Representatives presents the charges — a function similar to that of a grand jury — and the Senate sits as a court to try the impeachment. No impeached person may be removed without a two-thirds vote of the Senate. The Congress also plays a role in presidential elections. Both Houses meet in joint session on the sixth day of January, following a presidential election, unless by law they appoint a different day, to count the electoral votes. If no candidate receives a majority of the total electoral votes, the House of Representatives, each state delegation having one vote, chooses the President from among the three candidates having the largest number of electoral votes. The Senate, each Senator having one vote, chooses the Vice President from the two candidates having the largest number of votes for that office.